She'd been thinking about Brody and suddenly, she was seeing him.

And hearing him.

It wasn't possible. She was in shock. And pain. Her shoulder hurt like the devil. That was it.

She flashed the light again, being careful to keep it away from his eyes. The man's body was long and lanky, with narrow hips and a flat stomach. Nice wide shoulders. Strong chin.

Oh, no. She knew that chin.

"Brody?" she said, her voice squeaking.

Said chin jerked up and she caught the full impact of his hazel eyes. He looked her up and down and even knowing that it was so dark that he couldn't be seeing much, it had her wanting to run and hide. Thirteen years. And it felt as if it were yesterday.

"Evening, Elle," he said, his voice sounding strained. "I guess this just proves that no matter how bad things are, they can always get worse."

TRAPPED

—

BEVERLY LONG

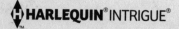

Recycling programs
for this product may
not exist in your area.

For my father, who was sent to Colorado
before he shipped out for WWII.
He learned to ski and fell in love!

ISBN-13: 978-0-373-74847-1

TRAPPED

Copyright © 2014 by Beverly R. Long

Printed in U.S.A.

ABOUT THE AUTHOR

As a child, Beverly Long used to take a flashlight to bed so that she could hide under the covers and read. Once a teenager, more often than not, the books she chose were romance novels. Now she gets to keep the light on as long as she wants, and there's always a romance novel on her nightstand. With both a bachelor's and a master's degree in business and more than twenty years of experience as a human resources director, she now enjoys the opportunity to write her own stories. She considers her books to be a great success if they compel the reader to stay up way past their bedtime.

Beverly loves to hear from readers. Visit www.beverlylong.com, or like her at www.facebook.com/beverlylong.romance.

Books by Beverly Long

HARLEQUIN INTRIGUE
1388—RUNNING FOR HER LIFE
1412—DEADLY FORCE**
1418—SECURE LOCATION**
1436—FOR THE BABY'S SAKE
1472—DEAD BY WEDNESDAY
1513—HUNTED§
1520—STALKED§
1526—TRAPPED§

**The Detectives
§The Men from Crow Hollow

CAST OF CHARACTERS

Elle Vollman—When her small plane crashes in the Amazon jungle, Elle must team up with Brody Donovan, the fiancé she ran away from thirteen years earlier. It would be too much to expect his forgiveness, but can she count on his help when it becomes apparent that a madman is determined that she's never going to make it out of the jungle alive?

Dr. Brody Donovan—When the plane crashes, Brody is able to render medical aid. But he can't stop his own blood pressure from rising when he realizes that he's stranded in the Amazon jungle with Elle Vollman, the only woman he's ever loved. Is he willing to risk his heart one more time?

Leo Arroul—He's been Elle's friend for years and she trusts him. Will he cross Jamas by helping Elle and Brody escape? Or is he already on Jamas's payroll?

Captain Ramano—He does a masterful job landing the plane in the jungle, but does he know more about the engine trouble than he's willing to share? Would he have deliberately crashed his own plane?

T. K. Jamas—He's a predator of young girls, luring them into the world of human trafficking. He will stop at nothing to ensure that Elle never testifies against him. But is the love he has for his mother his one vulnerability?

Felipe—He's T. K. Jamas's right-hand man but he has his own reasons for capturing Elle and Brody. To what lengths will he go to ensure that they cooperate with his plans?

Maria—She's a nurse and appears loyal to Jamas. Have Brody and Elle underestimated her ability to help or harm them?

Chapter One

Brody Donovan moved in his seat, trying to discreetly stretch his long legs. The pretty young woman across the aisle smiled at him.

"Long flight, huh?" she said.

Long, late and the last twenty minutes, bumpy as hell. He glanced at his watch, judging the amount of time he'd have between connecting flights. "Yes," he said politely, and promptly closed his eyes.

He didn't want to engage in any conversation. He wanted solitude. For the next ten days, he planned to enjoy the quiet and forget about the bang of roadside bombs, the sting of metal fragments and the despair of the damaged bodies that he'd been patching up for years. He intended to forget about war and to pretend that everybody *could just get along*.

His destination of choice involved a little backtracking, but he was okay with that. A direct flight out of Miami into Brasília, the

capital of Brazil, then a smaller plane to take
him an hour north to a place where the sand
was white, the water blue and the rum cold.

He had a place to stay, courtesy of his friend
Mack McCann. Payback, his friend had said
for Brody's assistance in saving Hope Minnow's life. After hearing that Brody had a trip
to South America in mind with no particular
destination, Mack had been quick to call in a
few favors and suddenly Brody had a beach
house in Brazil waiting for him.

Peace. A brief interlude before the real world
and its real-world responsibilities pressed down
upon him. It wasn't as if he was dreading the
next step. San Diego, with its three hundred
days a year of sunshine and mild temperatures,
wasn't something to bitch about. And he was
joining one of the leading orthopedic practices
in the country. It was just that…

Well, it was just that with both of his good
friends finding love, it was hard not to feel a
little alone. In just a few weeks, they would
both be married. Ethan to Chandler, Mack's
younger sister. And Mack to Hope Minnow,
who he'd been hired to protect and in the process, had lost his heart.

He should just be happy for both Ethan and
Mack and stop the damn pity party. It wasn't
his style. Marriage simply wasn't in the cards.

He'd come close, but Elle... Well, she'd walked away without a backward glance.

Those had been dark days. But he'd managed to go on even though some days he'd barely had the strength to get out of bed.

He would forget the bad stuff about war, too. Given enough time.

And plenty of rum.

Brody woke up when he felt the wheels touch down. The big plane taxied to a gate and the passengers shuffled restlessly, waiting for the doors to open. Once they did, it was straight to Customs. The fine folks there were moving at the pace of a comatose snail, and he checked his watch repeatedly. If he missed his next flight, it would mean a night in the airport.

Once past the Customs agent, he moved fast, looking for signs that would lead him in the right direction. Fortunately, everything was in both Spanish and English. He started running, being careful to dodge around the elderly and the very young. When he got to his gate, he wasn't surprised to see the waiting room was empty. There was a clerk behind the counter, fiddling with his computer. When the young, dark-skinned man saw him, he immediately glanced toward the big windows.

Brody followed his gaze. The small plane was still there, but they were starting to pull the temporary steps back. The propeller on the nose was turning.

The young man spoke into a microphone on his shirt collar. "One more," he said. Then he looked at Brody. "You just made it."

Brody held out his ticket and his passport. The young man hit a few keys. "Thank you, Señor Donovan. There are no assigned seats."

He knew that. It was a small chartered flight. The plane only held a max of eight.

"I'll hang on to the wing if I have to," he said. Warm sand, blue water and cold rum were a hell of an inducement.

The young man smiled. "I do not think that will be necessary." He opened a door and motioned for Brody to pass through. "Have a good trip," he said.

Brody moved quickly through the short hallway and took the steps down to the tarmac fast. He pushed open a big door and was outside. The air felt sticky even though there was a good breeze. It was darker than it should have been, given that it was still an hour shy of sundown.

Everything was gray. Gray cement. Gray plane. Gray sky.

He was pretty confident that the rain was not far off. That didn't worry him. In this part of the country, they had to be used to flying in it.

They didn't call it the rain forest for nothing.

He ran up the metal steps and ducked to enter the plane. Seated in the cockpit was a pilot, a man close to sixty with dark skin and still-thick dark hair, who didn't look up. The copilot, blond, blue-eyed and freckled, probably not yet twenty-five, reached back over his shoulder, grabbed Brody's ticket and then pointed a thumb to a seat in the empty front row. With the same arm, he pulled shut a curtain, separating the cockpit from the rest of the cabin.

Brody swung into the spot, silently celebrating his good luck, not caring that the pilot seemed a little irritated with his late arrival. In another hour, he'd be at his final destination. Mack had gone so far as to hire somebody to stock the house with groceries. All Brody had to do was show up.

The plane taxied out to a runway and within minutes was gathering speed. The nose of the plane lifted and suddenly they were airborne. The small aircraft rocked back and forth, causing Brody, who had been on some pretty rough flights during his years in the air force, to brace one hand on the wall and the other on the plastic armrest between his seat and the empty one next to it.

"I told you it would be bad," a woman said

from somewhere behind him. "You never listen to me."

There was a response. From a man. Too low for Brody to distinguish the words.

"This is the dumbest thing we've ever done," she added, evidently not letting it go.

Brody wished he'd remembered earplugs. The plane continued to gain altitude. And the flight didn't get any smoother. He understood. Planes like this flew at lower altitudes where the air was denser and rougher. They probably wouldn't go much higher than three or four thousand feet.

He closed his eyes.

Fifteen minutes later, the plane started to really rock and roll. He opened his eyes just as a bolt of lightning split the darkening sky off to his left.

More lightning followed.

He leaned into the aisle and looked toward the front. The curtain separating the pilots from the rest of the plane had slid partially open, allowing him to see. The older pilot was gesturing to the young copilot, his hands moving fast. It appeared that nerves up front were stretched thin.

He hoped the woman in back didn't have a good view. The man with her would never hear the end of it.

It probably wouldn't do any good to tell her that lightning wasn't going to bring down a plane. Hadn't happened for more than forty years. The skin of a plane was hyper conductive, causing any electrical charges to skate along the exterior of the plane and then to discharge back into the atmosphere.

Nope. Probably wouldn't make her any happier to know that.

He closed his eyes again, hoping they got out of the storm soon. But his eyes opened fast when he felt the plane start to lose altitude. What the hell? They were descending fast. Way too fast.

The young copilot stumbled out of the front. His face was pale and he was sweating. "Captain Ramano says to prepare for a crash landing."

ELLE VOLLMAN WASN'T prone to regrets, but when she realized the plane was going down, a few thoughts flashed through her terrified mind. Mia, sweet Mia. How could the little girl endure another loss? Elle had wanted so desperately to give her the life she deserved.

She would miss Father Taquero, too. He'd first become her friend, then her employer and, most recently, her confidant. Then he'd taken on his most important role—Mia's protector.

And then, of course, there was her biggest regret. Brody Donovan. The only man she'd ever loved. She wished she'd had the chance to tell him. Not that he'd probably have been interested in listening. He had to hate her for what she'd done.

She leaned forward in her seat, crossed her arms in front of her, bent her head and prepared to die. Her ears were roaring, her head was pounding and when the plane skimmed the first tree, she heard branches crack and bust and then the scream of metal tearing. The plane tossed from side to side, then rolled and rolled again.

Something hit her in the head, right above her left eye. She felt her seat belt give and she pitched sideways. Blindly, she reached out and grabbed air. Suddenly the plane came to a bone-jarring stop. She fell forward, catching her shoulder on the seat across from her. She felt it give and a searing pain stab at her.

She lifted her head. She felt sick and disoriented, and where the hell was the emergency lighting that every airline promised in the event of emergency? It wasn't pitch-black but pretty dark. She couldn't see much of anything.

A horrifying thought struck her. Maybe she was blind. Maybe the knock on her head had taken her sight. She was seconds away from full-blown panic when she remembered that she had a flashlight in her backpack. Keeping her injured arm anchored to her side, she used her other to claw around on the floor, feeling her way, until finally her outstretched fingers snagged a backpack strap. She pulled the heavy bag toward her and unzipped it. She reached in, past the extra clothes and the books that she carried with her.

There it was. She pulled out the light, turned it on and very quickly realized that sight wasn't always a gift.

It was a gruesome scene. The inside of the plane had been torn apart and strips of metal and chunks of glass were everywhere. There was a gaping hole in the roof at the very rear of the plane, less than three feet behind where she'd been sitting.

The elderly woman across the aisle was leaning back in her seat, her eyes closed, and blood was running down her face. Her husband was still bent over, in the crash position, with a section from the roof of the plane, probably four feet long and at least a foot wide, pressing on his back.

They were holding hands. And the man's thumb was stroking the woman's palm and her index finger was gently tapping on his gnarled knuckle.

It was witnessing that small connection that gave Elle the strength to move forward. She was alive. Others were alive. All was not lost.

She fished inside her backpack again and pulled out her cell phone. She turned it on, knowing it was a long shot. Still, when there was no service, she experienced a sharp pang of disappointment. She dropped it back into her backpack.

It felt surreal. Like one of those dumb movies where the world has ended and there's only a few mopes to carry on.

Get a grip, she lectured herself. The world hadn't ended, and she wasn't the only one left alive. She'd been in a plane crash. Nothing more. Nothing less.

And she needed to figure out what to do next.

The elderly couple was likely injured, but before she assisted them, she needed to determine how the rest of the passengers had fared. She flashed her light into the seats directly ahead of her. There had been a woman there. She'd had her face buried in a thick book when Elle boarded.

She was still there, her arms wrapped around her middle, silently rocking back and forth. Her eyes were wide-open. Blank.

"Are you all right?" Elle asked.

The woman slowly nodded. She did not make eye contact with Elle.

"What's your name?" Elle asked.

"Pamela," she said, her voice a mere whisper.

"Okay, Pamela, I'm going to check on the pilots. I'll be right back." Elle flashed the light forward to the front of the plane. In the aisle was someone's overnight bag, several magazines and other papers, a coat and more pieces of the plane's interior wall.

Elle stepped over the debris. When she stopped to yank back the partially closed curtain that separated the cockpit from the cabin, Pamela almost rammed into her back.

Elle understood. The need for human contact, to know that she wasn't alone, was almost overwhelming.

Elle could see that the pilot was still in his seat, slumped over the controls. The copilot had been thrown out of his seat and was awkwardly sprawled in the small space between the two seats. He was moving, thank God, picking himself up. Half-up, he suddenly crumpled on his right side. Arms flailing, he grabbed for his chair and sank down. "Oh, damn, that hurts," he said, reaching for his lower leg.

His hand came away with blood and Elle thought she might be sick. She forced herself to step closer.

The man had pulled up his loose pants, and sticking out of his lower leg was the sharp, ugly end of a bone. There was blood. It wasn't spurting out, like when Father Taquero had cut his hand at the church a month ago, but to her inexperienced eye, there did seem to be a rather lot of it.

"Don't move," she said instinctively.

"Not much chance of that," he said, his jaw tight. He turned his pale face to the man at his side. "Captain Ramano." His voice was a plea.

The older man groaned but didn't push his body back or lift his head.

They were both alive but certainly hurt.

"Can you call for help?" Pamela asked, over her shoulder, evidently not caring about their injuries.

To his credit, the young copilot fiddled with several switches. "No power," he said, his young voice showing the strain. "There's no radio." He pulled a cell phone from his back pocket and pressed a couple keys. "No signal."

"That's okay," Elle said, attempting to stay calm.

"It's not okay," Pamela said, her voice too loud for the small space. "I smell fuel. We're going to blow up. We have to get out. Now!"

Elle turned. She spoke with the authority that had always successfully quieted a room of preteen girls. "We will. Now, you need to stay calm and help me. We have to help the others."

Pamela pressed her lips together. Then she whirled suddenly, her arm flailing to the side. "What about him?" she asked, pointing to the front row. "Can he help?"

Elle had forgotten about the man who had boarded late. She'd been writing in her journal and had looked up just as he swung his body into the seat. She'd caught a glimpse of broad shoulders in a pale green shirt.

She turned back to the young copilot and swallowed hard. "I am going to help you." She wasn't sure how, but she would do something. "But first, I need to see how badly the rest of the passengers are injured. Can you hang on?"

He nodded and closed his eyes.

Elle turned and stepped past Pamela, to the point where she could shine the light on the remaining passenger's seat. Because the man had been in the front row, there hadn't been any seat for him to use to brace himself. It appeared as if his belt had failed, as hers had, and he'd been pitched out of his seat onto the floor. He was under debris from the wall and ceiling. She could see an arm, a leg, a portion of his back.

She let the light rest there. He was breathing. Alive. He moved his legs, then his arms.

"Be careful," she said. "You've got stuff on your back."

The man stilled.

"We'll try to lift it off," she said. She motioned for Pamela to help her. "I can only use one arm," she said to Pamela. "But between the two of us, we should be able to do it."

But she wasn't going to be able to hang on to her flashlight, and they couldn't work in the dark. She stepped toward the elderly woman. Now her eyes were open. Alert.

"My name is Elle," she said.

"I'm Mrs. Hardy," she said. "Beatrice Hardy. You need to help my husband."

"Go on, Bea," the elderly man said. "I'm not going anywhere."

Sort of what the copilot had said. "I'll help him," Elle promised. "But first we're going to help the man up front. I need you to hold the flashlight for us. Can you do that?"

The woman unbuckled her seat belt, got up and reached for the flashlight. They returned to the front of the plane. Working together, Elle and Pamela dug the man out, tossing the heavy pieces aside. It was wood or fiberglass or some other combination of materials, she wasn't sure. All she knew was that it was heavy and, while she kept her right arm tucked next to her side, it was impossible to keep the right side of her body from moving. Piercing pain traveling through her neck, shoulder and arm was the result. It made her feel sick to her stomach.

Finally, the man was free. She could hear him moving in his seat, but the light was not quite in the right spot. She retrieved the flash-light from Mrs. Hardy, who immediately re-turned to her husband's side, and aimed it toward the man.

Evidently right in his eyes.

"Hey," he said, protesting, holding his hand in front of his eyes.

She lowered the light fast.

And wondered if she'd been too quick to dis-miss her own head injury. She'd been think-ing about Brody and, suddenly, she was seeing him.

And hearing him.

It wasn't possible. She was in shock. And pain. Her shoulder hurt like the devil. That was it.

She flashed the light again, being careful to keep it away from his eyes. The man's body was long and lanky, with narrow hips and a flat stomach. Nice wide shoulders. Strong chin.

Oh, no. She knew that chin.

"Brody?" she said, her voice squeaking.

Said chin jerked up and she caught the full impact of his hazel eyes. He looked her up and down and even knowing that it was so dark that he couldn't be seeing much, she wanted to run and hide. Thirteen years. And it felt as if it were yesterday.

"Evening, Elle," he said, his voice sounding strained. "I guess this just proves that no matter how bad things are, they can always get worse."

Chapter Two

The minute he said it, he was sorry. Over the years, Brody had thought of a thousand things that he might say to Elle if their paths ever happened to cross. That had not been one of them.

He felt worse when he heard her quick intake of breath. And he was just about to apologize when she stepped toward him. "This is Pamela. Mr. and Mrs. Hardy, mid-seventies, are in the back row. Total of five passengers. Two crew. Copilot has a bone sticking out of his lower leg and the pilot is barely conscious and bleeding from the head. No working radio."

It was a nice, concise report but did nothing to explain why she was on this plane.

Damn, the side of his head hurt. When the plane was rolling, everything became a projectile and something had knocked into him pretty hard. He was pretty sure he'd lost consciousness briefly. When he was coming to, he'd heard Elle's voice, like so many times in his dreams. Then, when she moved closer to lift the weight off his back, and he'd smelled orange blossoms, he'd been shocked. Never before had Elle's sweet scent been part of his dreams.

Then she'd said his name and he about jumped out of his own skin.

How many times over the years had he heard her say *Brody?* Her tone rich, a little lower than the average woman's. In friendship—that had come first. In passion—it had followed pretty quickly. In joy—he liked to think so. Maybe he'd have heard it in sorrow when she left, but he'd never know. All he'd gotten was a note.

And now didn't exactly seem like the right time to ask for more information. Now was the time to do what he did best.

"Either of you injured?" he asked.

The woman next to Elle stepped forward. "We have to get out. You have to help us."

"Are you injured?" Brody repeated.

"No. I mean, I don't think so. We have to go now. The plane might explode."

Elle had introduced her. What was her name? "Pamela, right?"

"Yes."

"I want you to sit tight for just a minute." He turned his attention to Elle. "I heard you say something about your arm."

"It's fine," she said, dismissing the inquiry. "What about you?"

He rolled his shoulders back and considered his own injuries. He'd been lucky. He was going to have a hell of a lump on his head, but he could get past that. Something from above had hit his back and it was definitely going to be bruised and sore tomorrow, but if the angle of the hit had been a little sharper and a couple inches higher, it likely would have fractured his spine and he would never have walked again.

He stood up, careful not to hit his head on parts of the hanging interior. "I'm good to go. I'll check the crew first," he said.

She moved, shrinking far enough back in the small space to let him pass without touching her. He was grateful for that. His nerves felt pretty raw. When the copilot announced that they should prepare to crash, he'd prepared to die. Had said a quick prayer, said a mental goodbye to his parents and to both Ethan and Mack, the best friends a man could have had. And he'd thought about Elle, whom he'd loved and lost and never known why.

"I'll need some light," he said. She handed him the flashlight. He took it, careful not to brush up against her fingers.

He saw the young copilot sitting in his chair

and moved toward him. "My name is Brody Donovan. I'm a doctor," he said.

"Thank God, a doctor," the young man said, his jaw clenched tight. "I hope you don't deliver babies for a living."

"Orthopedic surgeon," Brody said.

"My lucky day," the copilot said.

Brody wasn't so sure of that. He'd seen enough to know that the young man had a compound fracture of the tibia.

"What's your name?" Brody asked.

"Angus Bayfield."

"Angus, I'm going to be able to help you, but for now, I need you to not move that leg." When a bone broke and one end protruded through the skin, that meant that there was another sharp end still inside the leg, able to do all kinds of damage to veins and arteries. The blood loss wasn't bad and he wanted to keep it that way.

"I'm going to quickly assess the others," Brody said. He'd been in a combat zone for a long time. Triage was the name of the game. Assess everyone, identify the wounded, identify those most *critically* wounded that would *benefit* from treatment, and proceed from there. "Are there any other flashlights on board and what about a first-aid kit?"

The man pointed over his shoulder toward

a big flashlight that was still miraculously hanging on the wall. Brody reached over and unsnapped the straps that kept it in place and flipped it on. It lit up the whole space, much better than the small flashlight that Elle had given him.

There were sections of the roof of the plane hanging down and exposed wires. The front windshield was shattered, making it difficult to see anything outside.

He heard movement behind him and turned. It was Elle. He handed her back her flashlight.

"I'm going to sit with the Hardys," Elle said.

"Tell them I'll be there in just a minute."

"Sir," Angus said, "there's a first-aid kit under the captain's seat."

Brody fished around and pulled out the rectangular aluminum box. Holding the flashlight in one hand, he used his other to flip open the lid. He made a quick assessment. Basic stuff. Bandages. Gauze. Alcohol sponges. Ibuprofen. Antiseptic wipes. Antibiotic ointment. Adhesive tape. Scissors. Several pairs of gloves.

He turned toward the pilot. The man was still strapped in and he was regaining consciousness. He pushed himself back from the controls, almost to the point where he was sitting up. He looked stunned. There was blood running down the side of his face from a hell of a gash on the side of his head where something had obviously hit him.

"I'm a doctor," Brody said, his voice gentle. "I can help you."

He lifted the man's wrist and took his pulse. Steady. Maybe a little slow but not alarmingly. He needed to get the bleeding stopped. "You've got a head injury. Are you in pain anywhere else?" he asked.

The man shook his head, very slowly. Brody didn't believe him. He wasn't confident the man even realized that he was a pilot and that his plane had just crashed in the Amazon jungle.

"What the hell happened?" Brody asked, turning towards the copilot.

"I'm not sure. There was some kind of malfunction with the electrical system. We lost power. Captain Ramano did a hell of a job keeping us out of a spin."

Captain Ramano didn't add anything to the conversation, confirming for Brody that he was definitely injured.

"The lightning?"

"I don't think so. I've flown through storms before with Captain Ramano and we've never had any trouble."

First time for everything. "Did you get a distress call through?"

"We did. Although I'm not sure how much good it will do. Even using satellite imaging, it's hard to find a plane in the rain forest."

He was probably right. Rain forests were known for their dense canopy of trees, and that would complicate an air search. But he couldn't focus on that right now.

"I'll be back," Brody said.

Pamela was sitting in the first row, staring at the door, looking as if she intended to make a break for it. He did not relish the idea of chasing after someone in the dark jungle. "Pamela, I need your help," he said.

She didn't answer but she did stand up. He led her back to the cockpit, where he opened the first-aid kit again, removed a wrapped gauze pad and opened it.

He motioned for her to get as close to the pilot as she could. "I need you to press this hard against that cut. Can you do that, Pamela?"

"I'm not touching blood."

He'd been just about to get to that. He pulled a pair of gloves out of the first-aid kit and handed them to Pamela. She hesitated and then put them on.

"Okay," he said. "Put pressure on and don't stop until I come back."

He shone his flashlight ahead of him. At the back of the small plane, Elle was kneeling next to the elderly couple. Her hair was still dark, cut shorter than it had been in college when she'd worn it past her shoulders. He could see her slender neck, her collarbone.

Elle had always been slim and in good shape. She'd been a good athlete, too. The bar where she'd worked had fielded a volleyball team that played on Sunday afternoons, and he'd loved watching her. So graceful yet she could jam the ball down an opponent's throat.

Now she had one arm out, patting the shoulder of Mrs. Hardy, who was talking a mile a minute. She had her other arm tucked into her side.

When she heard him moving down the aisle, she stepped aside.

The elderly woman stared at him. "My husband says it doesn't hurt, but he can't move. Please help him. You have to help him. We're on our fiftieth anniversary trip. He's—"

"I'm going to do everything I can," Brody said. He looked at the woman's cheek. She had a cut that was bleeding, but it didn't look deep. "But here's what I need from you. I want you to stand up and move to the other side of the plane. I'm going to need your spot."

The woman shut up now that she had some direction. She got out of her seat and stood next to Elle. That's when he realized that Elle also had blood on her face. And her eyes held the look of someone in pain.

He reached for her.

She jerked back.

"You're bleeding," he said.

"It's nothing. Help the others first."

He gave the cut on her forehead another look. Head wounds always bled a lot, and this one was no exception. But it appeared to have stopped bleeding. Still, there could be glass in it. He took a quick glance at her very brown eyes. Pupils were the same size.

"Him first," she said.

"Okay. But I'm going to look at that arm, too."

She nodded.

He stepped into the seat that Mrs. Hardy had vacated. It was awkward, but he got a good hold of the debris and shoved it away from her husband. He put a hand on the man's back, assuring him. "Don't move just yet," Brody said. He ran his hand down the man's spine. "Are you in pain?"

"No. Damn thing didn't hit me hard, thank goodness."

"Okay. Then try to sit back." The man had been very lucky. He was at an age when it became difficult to recover from severe injuries. When the man was upright, Brody took his pulse and used the flashlight to check his pupils. Both okay.

Brody stepped back. It was quite frankly amazing that everyone on board had survived the crash. He'd seen enough aircraft-crash-scene victims over the years to know that there were common injuries caused by the pressure of rapid descent. Vertebrae compression. Or a ring fracture at the base of the skull caused by force traveling through the spinal column. Sometimes even internal injuries caused by the jerk of the lap belt. Lower-limb injuries were common as legs flailed around and struck things, so Angus's fractured tibia didn't surprise him.

He'd set the leg as best he could. Unfortunately, however, what might be a relatively minor injury in a fully equipped operating room became potentially life threatening when there were nonsterile conditions and delayed treatment. And the humidity in this part of the world was a virtual breeding ground of bacteria.

He turned, only to realize that Elle had returned to the cockpit. She was talking to Angus, obviously trying to comfort him.

It was difficult to tell how badly the captain was hurt. Angus definitely needed the most immediate treatment, and there wasn't any room in the cockpit area to do that.

Elle saw him start back down the aisle and met him halfway. "What do you think?" she asked.

"On the plus side, I think Mr. and Mrs. Hardy are fine. They're probably going to be stiff and sore as the night wears on. The biggest risk for Pamela is to keep her from running off into the rain forest. You, I'd like to see that shoulder."

"I'm fine," she said.

He shook his head. When she'd moved out of the way earlier so that he could get to Mr. Hardy, he'd seen enough to realize that it wasn't her arm that was injured, but rather her shoulder. "Elle, please don't be stubborn about this. It's just wasting time. I'm going to need help with Angus and you're the only logical person to do it. I need you to have two arms and hands that are working."

It was the right approach. She clearly didn't want to impede the others receiving medical care.

She put her flashlight down and moved so that she stood in front of him. They were just inches apart and he was reminded of how nicely her head used to fit under his chin. He took a deep breath, put his hand on her shoulder joint and probed gently. "You dislocated your shoulder," he said.

"My seat belt broke," she said. "I got tossed out and hit the back of another seat with my shoulder."

"When you hit it, your humerus popped out of the shoulder socket. I can pop it back into place, but it's going to hurt. Maybe a lot."

She nodded. "Just get it over with."

Chapter Three

He stretched out her arm, raised it above her head and, at exactly the right spot, used the heel of his hand to pop the joint back into place.

She let out a hiss of air. He'd seen big, tough guys yelp when they experienced the same thing. "Okay?" he asked.

"Lovely," she managed.

He almost smiled. "I think it's possible that the captain has some internal injuries that we'll have to watch for. He probably hit the dash pretty hard. I'll bandage his head after I set the copilot's leg. Unfortunately for Angus, we don't have any ice and it's going to be difficult to keep the swelling down. His leg really needs stitches, but I didn't see any needles or thread in the first-aid kit. Same issue with Captain Ramano. I'd like to stitch up his head wound."

"I have a sewing kit," Elle said. "It's just a small one. I think it was a giveaway at a conference I attended a couple years ago and I toss it in my carry-on when I travel, just in case."

It was better than nothing. The needles wouldn't be nearly as sharp as what he was used to, but he could make them work. He could sterilize the needle and the thread with one of the antiseptic wipes in the first-aid kit. Not great but better than leaving a gaping wound. "Please get it," he said.

She found her bag in the rubble and dug through it, pulling out a tiny plastic box with three needles and six small coils of thread in it. She handed it to him.

"What else do you need me to do?" she asked.

The Elle he remembered had turned a little green when he discussed the surgeries he was observing in medical school. "There's going to be blood," he said.

"I'll be okay," she said, swallowing hard.

He studied her. So familiar. Yet so different. It was hard to get his head around it, so he did what was simple. He pushed it to the back of his mind. There were wounded. That's where his energies needed to be.

"Okay. Clear some space in the aisles. It's the only place where there will be room to work. I really need something to..." He let his voice trail off. He saw something that would work.

In Mr. Hardy's seat pocket, there were several newspapers. Brody grabbed one and handed it to Elle. "Once the space is clear, lay this down on the floor."

He was going to need something to sop up the blood, especially if he got unlucky and the sharp edges of bone cut a vein or an artery.

"If I only had a scalpel, I'd be in good shape," he said, under his breath.

Mrs. Hardy pointed to one of the large suitcases that had spilled out of the cabinet. "I've got a knife in with my makeup. Never gets caught by airline security."

Brody figured security had seen it but just decided they didn't want to have the twenty-minute conversation with Mrs. Hardy about why she had to fly with a knife. He opened the suitcase. Mrs. Hardy's makeup was in the zipper pocket. He was surprised when he saw the lovely pearl-handled instrument, tucked in beside lipsticks and powders. He'd expected something like a butter knife or at best a little pocketknife. No. Mrs. Hardy was *packin'*. Fully unfolded, the knife had at least a three-inch blade. The woman could have done some serious damage with it.

Brody looked from the knife to Mrs. Hardy and then back again. "And I had to give up my four ounces of shaving cream," he said.

Mrs. Hardy smiled. "There are advantages to being an old woman."

Brody tested the point against the palm of his hand. It was very sharp and would make a difference. "Thank you," he said, and started for the cockpit.

When Brody got there, Angus had his head back and his eyes were closed. Captain Ramano also had his eyes shut. Pamela was wide-awake and looking pretty agitated.

She was still dutifully pressing down on the pilot's head wound. "How is he?" Brody asked.

"I don't know. I'm not the doctor," she said crossly.

"You're doing fine," Brody assured her. "The bleeding looks as if it has stopped. You can go back to your seat."

He'd assist Captain Ramano once he finished with Angus. He tapped the young man on the shoulder. Angus opened his eyes.

"So it wasn't a dream?" Angus said.

Brody shook his head. "Wish it was, my friend. Once we get that leg set, you'll feel better. I promise."

He helped Angus up out of his seat. There was so little room that as careful as they were, at one point Angus brushed his injured leg against something and let out a yelp as if he were an injured dog.

The young man leaned heavily on Brody as they carefully maneuvered back to the main cabin area, where Brody helped him lie down. Angus wasn't a big guy, but he filled the small center aisle, and right now he looked as if he was about ready to pass out. His pant leg was still rolled up and Brody got his first really good look at the leg. It was already starting to swell. Brody untied the man's shoe and took it off.

It was going to get worse before it got better. This was frontier medicine and he didn't even have any rotgut whiskey to give to Angus.

Elle took a spot on one side, Brody on the other, each of them shoehorned in the seating area. Both were on their knees.

She could see the pain on Angus's face and she looked up at Brody. "He's lucky you were on this plane," she said.

He didn't answer her.

When Brody didn't answer, Elle realized that the young man she'd loved was gone. Instead, there was a stranger, who didn't feel the need to be particularly polite to her.

The Brody Donovan she remembered was always polite. She'd met him during his first year of med school. Had known he was supersmart after an hour of conversation, not because he told her he was—he just was. She'd enjoyed it when he and his friends came into the little bar where she'd been cocktailing. And when he asked her out, it had been flattering.

She'd declined. Men like Brody Donovan were out of her league. But he hadn't given up. Finally, she'd agreed, thinking it might be a nice holiday romance, and to her great surprise, and great joy, it had worked. They had clicked.

Loved the same movies, enjoyed the same food, laughed at the same things. She hadn't been a bit surprised when she learned that he'd been an Eagle Scout in middle school and the senior class president in high school. When he casually mentioned that his father was a novelist, she'd rather belatedly put together that Larry Donovan, hottest thriller writer around, was Brody's dad. Learning that his mother was a scientist who worked off and on for NASA didn't even make her blink an eye.

Brody was special.

When he graduated from med school with honors and had been accepted into his first choice for a residency program, everybody had assumed that he was rightfully on his way.

Everybody loved Brody. And she had, too. Which had made leaving him the hardest thing she'd ever had to do.

Brody opened the sewing kit, threaded a

needle with a piece of dark blue thread and set it down on the spread newspaper.

He opened a couple packages of antiseptic wipes, then handed her a pair of gloves and slipped a pair onto his own hands. "Angus, I'm going to move your bone back into position. To do that, I'm going to make a very small incision, but given that I don't have anything to numb the pain, it's going to hurt. I need you to keep the leg as still as you possibly can. Can you do that for me?"

Brody's voice was calm, reassuring.

Angus nodded.

"Elle, wipe that blood away," Brody said, his voice still calm.

She took the antiseptic wipe and as gently as possible, tried to clean around the wound so that Brody could see what he was doing. Her stomach was jumping.

"After that, I'll be ready to stitch up the wound and bandage it. You'll be on the road to recovery. How's that sound, Angus?" Brody asked.

He got a nod from the man.

"Okay," Brody said, his voice soft. He wiped the knife off, using two more antiseptic pads.

With confidence that she could only imagine, he made a small incision on Angus's leg.

The young copilot jerked and moaned but kept his leg fairly still.

Then, using his hands, Brody pressed on the protruding bone and eased it back inside the leg. He was concentrating fiercely and she knew that he was trying to align the two sections of snapped bone so that healing could begin.

"It's going fine," he said, smiling at Angus.

The young man nodded and closed his eyes.

She'd always assumed that Dr. Donovan would have a good bedside manner. So confident, so smart. So calm.

Once Brody seemed satisfied with the position of the bone, he looked up at her. "Wipe off the needle and the thread with the antiseptic wipes."

She did as instructed and then handed him the needle.

"Thank you," he said automatically. "I need you to gently press the edges of the wound together while I stitch it up." That part seemed to go relatively well. The stitches closing up the incision were a nice straight line. When he got to the torn jagged edges of skin where the bone had poked through, they weren't quite as pretty.

Still, Brody looked satisfied when he put the needle back down on the newspaper. The wound was closed and the bleeding had stopped. He opened the tube of antibacterial cream and spread a liberal amount over the whole area. Then it was a bandage and some tightly wrapped gauze.

Brody took off his gloves and dropped them on the newspaper, then patted Angus's shoulder. "All done."

"Thank you," the young man whispered.

Elle didn't need a medical degree to know that she'd just witnessed something amazing.

"Now what?" she asked.

"I need to find something to immobilize the leg, to give the bones a chance to knit together."

His gaze settled on Mrs. Hardy's dark suitcase. It was still open from when he'd gone looking for the knife. The suitcase was a roller, with a nice sturdy handle. He ran a hand down the back of the suitcase before he looked up at Mrs. Hardy, who had been watching the entire process with Angus. "I might be able to use this," he said.

"Take what you need out of it," Mrs. Hardy said.

"It's not quite that easy," he said. "I hate to do this, but I'm going to need to tear the bag apart. I can use the two rods that connect to the handle."

Mrs. Hardy shrugged as if to say that she

and her husband had survived a plane crash and she didn't intend to sweat the small stuff.

Brody used Mrs. Hardy's knife to cut through the fabric, exposing the rods. Elle wasn't an expert, but they looked perfect. At least twenty inches long with a plate that attached them at the bottom. There were screws that connected the plate to the wheel assembly and another set of screws that fixed the rods to the handle.

Elle leaned toward the young pilot. "Angus," she said softly, "do you have any tools on board, like a screwdriver?"

"No, I don't think so."

Brody was already using the end of the knife to turn the screws. It was slow going, but he was making progress. Finally, the rods were loose. He looked up. "I need some strips of cloth."

"I've got T-shirts in my bag, young man," Mr. Hardy said. He pointed to a small bag that matched Mrs. Hardy's. It had somehow ended up near the front of the plane.

Brody opened the suitcase and pulled out several white T-shirts. He cut one into strips and used two more to wrap around the metal rods.

Then he put the padded rods in place, one of each side of Angus's leg. The metal plate at the end of the rods fit underneath Angus's foot.

Then Brody efficiently used the strips of T-shirt to tie everything tight. When he finally sat back to inspect his work, Elle could tell that he was pleased. He patted Angus's shoulder. "We're going to help you get up. You can take a seat in that last row so that you can keep your leg extended straight."

It was awkward, but between the two of them, they managed to get Angus up from the floor and onto a seat. There were beads of sweat running down the young man's face by the time they were finished.

"Thanks, Doc," he said.

"You're welcome," Brody said, smiling.

"I'm worried about Captain Ramano," Angus said. "I don't think he's doing so good."

"Don't worry," Brody assured him. "I'm going to check him next. First I'm going to elevate your leg a little. Just stay still." He grabbed several magazines that were lying around, stacked them and slid them under Angus's foot. Then he pulled a small foil-wrapped package of ibuprofen out of the first-aid kit. "Take a couple of these. It will help with the discomfort."

Elle reached for her backpack and pulled out a bottle of water that she'd bought at the airport after she got through security. She handed it to Angus.

Angus braced himself up on one elbow and took a big drink.

"Better save some of that for later," Brody cautioned.

The passengers all looked at each other. They heard the unspoken warning. *We may be here awhile and we don't want to run out of water.*

Pamela stepped forward. "Someone needs to be in charge of supplies. I'll do it."

Everyone was looking at Brody. He'd become the leader of the group, whether he wanted the post or not. "That's a good idea, Pamela," he said. "I suggest everybody throw in what you've got in your bags and we'll take an inventory. Just in case," he added.

Rather optimistically, Elle thought. She'd been living in this part of the world for several years. Planes didn't frequently crash in the jungle, but when they did, sometimes it took weeks to find the wreckage.

"I'm going to stitch up Captain Ramano's head wound," Brody said.

Elle swallowed hard. She'd gotten a look at that cut. "Do you need help?" she forced herself to ask.

Brody shook his head. "I'll manage," he said. "Do you think you could clean up Mrs. Hardy's cut on her face?"

She was getting the better end of the deal. "Of course."

"If there's any glass, leave it and I'll remove it," he said.

Elle didn't see any glass or anything else in Mrs. Hardy's cut. She cleaned it with an antiseptic wipe, smeared antibiotic cream on it and covered it with a small bandage. She could handle this kind of first aid. There was always some kid at the school getting a scraped knee or a skinned elbow.

She was almost done when Mrs. Hardy turned her head to look at her. "Do you and Dr. Donovan know each other?"

"Uh…why do you ask?"

"Well, I don't mean to be a meddling old lady, but I heard what he said. He didn't sound very happy to see you. And you looked very surprised to see him."

"We knew each other a long time ago. It's been thirteen years since we saw each other."

"Did you work together?"

"No. We were…" Friends. Lovers. For a minute, she considered lying about it. But she'd stopped running from the truth some time ago. "We were engaged," she said. "And I broke off the engagement."

"Gracious."

Indeed. "I'd appreciate it if you could keep

that information to yourself," Elle said. "We've got our hands full here and I don't want it to be a distraction."

Mrs. Hardy nodded. "It's not easy to be young," she said.

She had been young and probably immature. But she'd made the right decision. For Brody.

Who was returning from the cockpit. "How's Captain Ramano?" she asked.

"Conscious. I got his head wound cleaned up and stitched. I suspect he has a concussion and I'm still worried that there may be some internal injuries."

She looked around. The others were huddled around Angus, quietly conversing. "If you're right and he has internal injuries, he might not survive the night," she said.

"I'll watch him," Brody said. "These just aren't great conditions to have to cut someone open and try to stop internal bleeding."

"You would do that?" she asked.

"I'll do what I have to do," Brody said simply. "Right now I think we need to concentrate on that," he said, pointing to a hole in the roof of the plane. It was almost as if the hard impact had ripped apart a seam.

But it hadn't ripped neatly—the area around the hole was a jagged mess of metal. "We need to get that covered, but first, I'd like to use the hole to take a look around outside. I need something to stand on."

"There are some boxes in the closet at the front, the one where the flight crew hangs their jackets," Elle said.

"An empty box won't work," he said.

"They're not empty," Elle said.

He walked toward the closet, kicking additional debris out of his way as he went. He opened the closet door and, sure enough, there were two boxes. He picked one up. It was heavy. "What the heck is in here? Cement?"

"Books," Elle said.

He carried a box and set it down under the hole. The floor was wet and more water was dripping in. He got the second box. "I hope you don't mind if they get wet," he muttered.

"Under the circumstances, I think I can get past it," she said, her tone dry.

"People can get past a lot," he said to no one in particular. He stood on the boxes and carefully stuck his head outside. Rain pelted his face and shoulders. It was very dark and the moist smell of wet foliage was almost overwhelming. He raised his arm and shone his flashlight out into the distance.

Trees. And more trees. He pivoted, carefully moving his feet so as to not lose his balance on the stacked boxes. Every direction was the same. When he brought the light in closer, he could see where the plane had knocked through some trees, breaking off branches before it had come to rest on the floor of the jungle. The trees, big and leafy, towered over the plane, probably some seventy to eighty feet in the air.

Angus had been right. It was going to be very difficult for rescuers to find the plane.

ELLE REALIZED SHE'D been holding her breath while Brody was surveying the outside. When he pulled his torso and head back inside, she gulped in a big lungful of air.

"Well?" she asked.

For a minute, she thought he was going to tell her to look for herself. Then he let out a soft sigh, as if in acceptance that he was going to have to talk to her, regardless of how distasteful it might be.

"I don't think we're in any immediate danger," he said. "The plane appears to be on a flat surface. It's hard to see much, but I'm fairly confident of that. I think we need to sit tight tonight. I suspect they'll suspend any search until daylight."

She looked at her watch. Daylight was ten hours away. "We should probably cover this hole," she said. "No need to advertise that there's fresh meat in the jungle," she said, attempting to insert a hint of levity into her tone.

He didn't smile. "I agree. If nothing else, we need to keep the mosquitoes out as best we can."

He was right. She'd had a malaria vaccine, but there wasn't one for dengue fever or several of the other diseases that mosquitoes carried. "There are some blankets in the front cabinet."

"I saw that, but let's see if we can find something else. We should reserve the blankets for warmth."

She started looking around. The plane was small with few hidden cracks or crannies. Behind the last row of seats was a built-in cupboard for passenger luggage with a double door. Both doors had come open during the crash and the few pieces of luggage inside had spilled out. On the shelf above the open space was…something. Whatever it was, it was covered in dust. Rather gingerly, she reached for a corner and pulled it toward her. With it halfway out, she realized what it was. She held it up for Brody and the others to see. "Look. A parachute."

"I think it's a little too late for that, dear," Mrs. Hardy said, humor in her tone.

Elle smiled at the woman. She didn't miss

the odd look in Brody's eye. He was probably thinking that she was pretty good at bailing out.

"This makes no sense," Elle said. "This is not the kind of plane you'd jump from."

Brody nodded. "You're right. It looks as if it got stuffed in here and somebody forgot about it. Regardless, it's a good find and quite frankly, we're due some luck."

Elle pulled the parachute out, spreading the nylon canopy as best she could in the small space. "I think this is a job for Mrs. Hardy's knife."

It took Elle several minutes to slice a section of the fabric that would cover the hole. When she was done, she looked up. That had been the easy part. Now she was going to have to go outside, climb on top of the plane and place it over the hole. She was worried about the jagged pieces of metal piercing the nylon, but she couldn't do much about that right now. Also, she'd have to find something heavy enough to lay over it to keep it in place. Maybe a few branches from some trees or even some heavy palm leaves. She could use Mrs. Hardy's knife to cut them off. "I'll go outside and put it over the hole."

"You're not going outside and climbing on top of this plane," Brody said, his tone adamant, as if it were the dumbest thing he'd heard today.

"Getting the hole covered is important," she reminded him.

"Cover it from the inside."

"I need tape and nails for that," she said. "I haven't come across any of that."

"There's some bandage tape in the first-aid kit. That should be strong enough to hold it."

"Shouldn't we save that, just in case?"

"It was a new roll," he said. "If you use some, we should still be okay." He walked toward her, first-aid kit in hand.

"How's the shoulder?" he asked.

"Fine. Good as new," she said.

"Okay. I want to clean up your head wound."

She let out a huff of air. "Fine."

He opened the first-aid kit and motioned for her to have a seat. Holding a flashlight in one hand and alcohol sponges in the other, he quickly cleaned and disinfected the wound. She tried to hold very still.

Brody Donovan had always had nice hands. Gentle. Yet strong.

There were no rings on any fingers. Was it even possible that he'd never married? Married and divorced? She doubted that. Once Brody made a promise, he'd keep it.

Unlike her.

"The cut is about an inch long but not too deep. I'm going to cover it. If you can keep it from getting infected, it will heal and probably won't even leave a scar."

She wasn't worried about a scar. She knew that small imperfections like that hardly mattered. "It will give me character," she said, trying to make light of the situation.

"You have a tan," Brody said, surprise in his voice.

She felt her whole body heat up. He used to tease her that her fair skin would never tan. On the other hand, she'd called him *Goldenboy*. He'd always been perpetually tanned from all his outdoor activities. That, combined with his light brown hair, which was naturally streaked with some lighter blond, and he looked as if he'd stepped out of a California tourism advertisement.

And while his hair was shorter than it had been in med school, he still looked very much the same. What had he been doing for the past thirteen years? And what had led him to be on a small charter plane in Brazil?

She had a thousand questions and no right to ask any of them.

Chapter Four

They found a total of four blankets. Brody gave one to the Hardys and one to Elle, who immediately offered to share with Pamela. The third he used to cover up Captain Ramano, who had finally gotten out of his seat and moved back into the main cabin area with the rest of them. The fourth went on top of Angus, who was restless with pain.

For himself, Brody pulled an extra shirt out of his bag and put it on. He was too wired to sleep and the jungle was anything but quiet at night. Even though Elle had done a good job covering the hole in the roof of the plane, all kinds of sounds still floated in.

He'd thought he'd be listening to the sound of surf outside his bedroom window tonight. Instead, he was listening to who knows what. The only given was that it likely wanted to eat him.

At the crack of dawn, he was going to build

a fire. That would make it easier for a search plane to locate them. He hoped the winds were light; otherwise the smoke would dissipate too fast. They did have one other weapon in their arsenal. Angus had said that there were some emergency flares. So, if a plane got close, they'd send up one of those.

Pamela snored, so around three in the morning, Elle threw back her portion of the blanket and walked over to sit in a seat on the other side of the cabin. It wasn't as if she could go far. The plane was not that big.

Brody watched her. She ignored him even though he was pretty sure she knew he was awake.

Which, for some crazy reason, rattled his chain. "So, what's with the books?" he asked.

It took her so long to answer he began to think that she wouldn't. No skin off his back.

"I teach English at a girls' school. These were extra books that we received. A priest that I know has a brother who is a teacher in Fortaleza at a very poor school. I offered to share the books with him."

"Couldn't you have shipped them?"

"Of course. But I was headed this direction anyway and I've gotten to know him, too, over the past couple of years. I was going to stay overnight with him and his wife before going on."

Before going on? "Where's your final destination?"

"Back to the States," she said, finally look at him.

"Really?" He paused. "For good?"

She shrugged. "I don't know. Things are… complicated."

He waited, hoping she'd tell him more. But she stayed quiet and his mind went about six directions.

Complicated because she was leaving a man? Leaving a family? Complicated because she no longer had a job? Complicated because she was on the run from the government? Complicated because she was part of the witness-protection program? Each thought was becoming more and more bizarre. He needed to stop.

They didn't owe each other any explanations. They were strangers who, a very long time ago, had had a moment.

A moment that had lasted two years.

A moment that had ended so fast that his head had whirled for months.

It had been thirteen years since he saw her. They'd met two years before that. He'd been in the middle of his second year of med school. She'd been a waitress in a little bar where the med students hung out. She'd been beautiful and articulate and very sexy in her short black skirt and white shirt. And she'd seemed to enjoy their brief conversations as he tried to devise ways to stretch out ordering a beer.

It had taken him six weeks and four invitations before she'd agreed to go out with him.

He'd relentlessly pursued her and pretty soon, they'd been spending all their free time together. On Christmas Eve, almost exactly two years after their first date, he'd asked her to marry him. When she'd said yes, he'd known it would be the best Christmas ever. They'd planned an early June wedding. In February, she'd bought a dress, which she refused to show him, saying it was bad luck. In March, they'd created a small guest list of close friends and family, which grew exponentially bigger when his parents had added their friends and extended family. As the list grew bigger and bigger, he'd noticed Elle's nervousness increase.

Don't be concerned about the expense, he'd told her. While it might have been traditional that the bride's parents paid for the wedding, he knew that Elle's mother was divorced. He suspected resources were limited. He'd encouraged her to add more guests from her side of the family, but she'd simply smiled and said that there was no one else.

They'd registered for wedding gifts, spending time he didn't have selecting china patterns and silverware. But he'd been happy enough to go without sleep. Nothing mattered except marrying Elle.

In the middle of April, eight weeks before the wedding, the invitations had gone in the mail and he'd arranged for Ethan and Mack to get fitted for tuxes.

On May 10, he'd walked out to get the mail, never anticipating that his life was about to change, that nothing would ever be the same, that nothing would ever be quite right again.

He'd seen the letter and had recognized the handwriting. Under a warm spring sun, wearing his pajama pants and his favorite Notre Dame sweatshirt, he'd opened the letter, thinking she'd probably sent him a funny card.

He'd read it twice. Nothing funny about it.

It had been full of apology. Full of a bunch of junk about how he'd be better off without her.

He'd run back into the house and frantically dialed the phone. She hadn't answered. He'd jumped in his car and gone to her apartment. Again, no answer. He'd found the landlord and given him a hundred bucks to open the door. Her clothes and personal things were gone.

He'd gone to Elle's workplace, but nobody had talked to her. Her boss, a man younger than

Brody, seemed more concerned about how he was going to fill her shifts than that she was missing. He'd turned to her family only to realize, rather belatedly, that he didn't even have her mother's number.

With the help of his family's attorney, he tracked down Elle's mother in a small town in central Utah. It had been a horribly awkward conversation. He'd said his name, expecting some sign of recognition. But there had been none. And it had quickly become apparent that Elle and her mother were not close when her mother had finally said that she hadn't heard from her daughter in months.

She'd also said she didn't understand why her daughter always had to be difficult.

The Elle he had known hadn't been difficult, but he was rapidly coming to the conclusion that he likely hadn't really known Elle.

The attorney had gotten the name of the stepdad through the divorce papers that were filed with the county. Even though Elle had never talked about her stepfather, Brody had contacted the man, who was living in Kentucky. Brody had left a message on the phone for the man, didn't get a call back for days, and finally when he followed up again, the man had said he wouldn't bother to open the door if Elle Vollman came knocking.

He'd called the police. They'd read the letter and looked at him with sad eyes and said there didn't appear to be much they could do.

He'd thought about hiring a private investigator. After all, people couldn't just disappear. He got as far as dialing the number one day. What stopped him was knowing that Elle hadn't disappeared. No. She'd left. Packed her bags and left.

Pride kept him from chasing after her.

But it had not kept him from holding his breath every damn day in anticipation of going to the mailbox. It had not kept him from being neurotic about making sure that his phone was charged.

After about a year, he'd stopped expecting her to make contact. At three years, he even got into the habit of not looking at his mail for weeks at a time.

At five years, he'd been able to think about it and not get sick. And within the last couple of years, he'd actually thought he was over it.

Now he knew he was wrong about that.

"Do you still keep in contact with Ethan and Mack?" she asked.

His friends had liked Elle. Had said that she

was a good match for him. They weren't generally so wrong. "I do. They're both getting married this summer. In just a few weeks, actually."

She pulled back in surprise. "No way."

"Yes. Ethan is marrying Chandler McCann, Mack's little sister. They reunited at the cabin last fall when somebody was trying to kill Chandler. Ethan wasn't having any of it. And Mack met Hope Minnow when he had a couple free weeks between leaving naval intelligence and starting a new job. Her dad is a television preacher and he and his family had been receiving some anonymous threats. Turned out there were a bunch of snakes in that crowd."

"Hope Minnow," Elle repeated. "Oh, yeah. I remember. I read an article about her in *People*. I suspect most men only looked at the pictures."

"Gorgeous and nice. Same for Chandler. My friends both got lucky."

She sat quietly for a long time with her eyes closed and he thought that she'd maybe fallen asleep. She surprised him when she turned to him. "Did you ever marry, Brody?"

He shook his head. "You?" he asked, and cleared his throat because his damn voice squeaked.

"No," she whispered.

He closed his own eyes. *Ask her why. Ask her*

why she left you. The voices in his head were hammering to be let out.

He kept his mouth shut. He'd survived a plane crash. He wasn't sure he could survive hearing her say that she just hadn't loved him enough.

He listened to her even breathing and pretty soon, he was confident that she was asleep.

Only then did he relax enough to drift off and catch a few hours of badly needed rest.

WHEN ELLE WOKE UP, she was sweating. The interior of the plane was warm. She looked around. Pamela and the Hardys were still sleeping. Angus was in his spot, his leg stretched out, his shoulders twitching in restless sleep. Captain Ramano was… Yikes, he was staring at her. When their eyes met, the captain quickly lowered his gaze. The previous night he'd been almost uncommunicative and she'd wondered if he wasn't in shock.

"How do you feel?" she whispered.

"My head hurts," he said. His voice was low, rusty from little use.

She smiled. "I'll bet it does. I'm sure help will come today. Do you remember what happened?" she asked gently.

He shrugged, then winced when that evidently hurt. "We started losing power in our engines. I did the best I could to get us down. It sure as hell wasn't *my* fault."

She wasn't imagining the emphasis on the one word. Who said something like that unless there was someone else that deserved the blame?

Had the plane been tampered with? Did he suspect that? Who would do something like that?

A chill ran down her spine. She knew someone who likely had the means to do something like that. Someone who hated her. Someone who would do most anything to make sure that she never reached the United States.

T. K. Jamas.

He was evil but was he crazy? Would he bring down a plane with innocent people on board just to harm her?

She had to know. "I'm not sure I understand what you mean by that," she said, her voice still a whisper. She didn't want anyone to overhear. "Whose fault is it?"

He stared at her. "How would I know?" he asked.

It wasn't an answer. And despite his head injury, she wanted to shake it out of him. "But the way you said…" She stopped. Brody stood in the doorway of the plane, his frame backlit by a streak of early-morning sunshine that had managed to make its way to the jungle floor. It caught the shine of his hair, the width of his shoulders.

He'd changed clothes. Instead of the cargo shorts he'd worn last night, he'd changed into jeans and a T-shirt. He had boots on his feet instead of sandals, and his jeans were tucked into the boots. It wasn't a great fashion statement but a good idea in the jungle where there were poisonous things crawling everywhere.

"Good call on the boots," she said, turning away from Captain Ramano.

"I threw them in at the last minute," he said, shaking his head. "I always loved hiking in Colorado and knew there were some mountains fairly close to my destination."

Elle wished she'd thought to bring boots. She had the loafers she was wearing and a pair of water shoes. At least she had on pants and a long-sleeved shirt over her cami. Her skin was mostly covered, which could be helpful in the jungle.

Brody walked over to Captain Ramano and looked at his eyes. Then he took his pulse and checked the bandage on his head wound. "I think you may have a slight concussion," he said. "Don't move around any more than you have to."

"I guess it was our lucky day that we had a physician on the plane," Captain Ramano said.

Brody shook his head. "It was our lucky day that you managed to land the plane without it being scattered around the jungle floor. We're going to get out of here. All of us."

Pamela stretched and then stood up. Her hair was going every direction. "They better find us today. We could starve. We have very little water and almost no food."

Mr. and Mrs. Hardy looked at each other. Brody shook his head. "We aren't going to starve. We may get a little hungry, but nobody has ever died from that. We'll have to be careful with our water."

Elle knew exactly how much water they had. And it wasn't enough. They would make it through today, but by tomorrow, they would need more. There was the bottle that Angus had drunk out of. The Hardys both had water bottles and Captain Ramano had had a large thermos of water wedged under his seat. Pamela had a sports drink.

Fortunately, water was generally readily available in the jungle. Unfortunately, it wasn't safe to drink. Unless it was boiled.

She watched Brody inspect the assortment that Pamela had gathered the night before. Four breakfast bars, a sack of chips, a can of mixed nuts, beef jerky, cheese popcorn and twelve tea bags.

"Who had the tea bags?" he asked.

Mrs. Hardy raised her hand. "A good cup of tea always makes me feel a little more civilized."

Elle didn't know about that. T. K. Jamas always drank tea. The first thing she'd noticed about the man was that he always had a cup of tea. He'd arrive at the school, cup in hand.

It made her sick to think that on more than one occasion she'd brewed him a fresh cup.

Brody smiled. "My mother always travels with tea bags. Says she can get through anything with a cup of tea."

"Smart woman," Mrs. Hardy said.

"Very. Anybody allergic to nuts?" Brody asked.

Everyone shook their heads.

"Okay," he said, "then I recommend we take a couple breakfast bars and some nuts, divide them up and save the remainder for later."

Pamela split two breakfast bars into seven equal pieces. It didn't take very long to distribute the portion, along with a handful of nuts, to each person. It took even less time for everyone to consume the meager breakfast. Still, Elle knew they were lucky to have something. It was supposed to be a short flight and she hadn't thought to pack any treats. However, she'd been able to contribute the breakfast bars because they'd been at the bottom of her backpack from a school excursion she'd had the prior week.

Brody made a special point to make sure that Angus ate and that he took some more ibuprofen for his pain.

"I'm going to get a fire going," Brody said.

"How are you going to manage that?" Pamela asked crossly.

Brody smiled congenially, choosing to ignore the testiness of Pamela's inquiry. "I was a Boy Scout. I know how to create friction and generate a spark."

Captain Ramano reached into his pocket. He pulled out two matchbooks, tossing one in Brody's direction. "This might make it easier."

Elle, who had wanted to shake the man five minutes ago, now wanted to hug him. The ability to make fire could be the difference in them surviving.

"Lots easier," Brody said, opening up the flap to show a half-full matchbook. "Someone will see our smoke and help will come."

There was no reaction from the group. Either they were afraid to jinx it by saying anything or they just didn't want to burst the good doctor's bubble.

Brody walked back outside. Pamela worked on the knots in her hair and Mrs. Hardy helped Mr. Hardy change his shirt.

Elle smeared some bug repellant from one of the two small tubes in her backpack on her bare ankles, her hands and neck before following Brody outside. She wanted to see the area in the light of day.

There were parts of the Amazon that you dared not venture into without a sharp machete because the massive undergrowth made walking almost impossible. In other parts, the undergrowth was almost nonexistent because of the thick canopy of trees that blocked any sunlight from hitting the jungle floor.

Where they had landed was sort of a hybrid of the two. There were trees of varying heights. Palms with big leaves, some just a few feet taller than her, some stretching another ten to twelve feet. There were kapok trees, one of the few she was familiar with because they grew so extensively in the Amazon. With a relatively skinny trunk, the tree could grow hundreds of feet. There were plants, big and bright green, some with beautiful flowers, ranging from knee-high to above their heads. In the spots where there weren't plants, the floor of the jungle was a tangle of wet dirt and short, mossy-looking grass.

It was in one long stretch of dirt and grass that Captain Ramano had managed to land the plane. It was a flat-out miracle. She stole a look at Brody's face and thought that he was thinking the same thing.

"You might want to put some of this on," she said, offering him the tube.

He looked at it. "Nice," he said.

"Yeah. I only threw a couple small tubes in my backpack. I thought I was going to be out of the jungle by tomorrow. If we don't have some on, the bugs will eat us alive."

He carefully put a little dab in his hand and smeared it on his exposed skin. She watched him rub his neck, watched the smooth motion of the hand that had tickled her in fun, stroked her in passion.

She looked away.

From the corner of her eye, she watched him approach a midsize kapok tree that had fallen, likely some time ago. It had probably been hit by lightning. There were long branches at the end that extended wide on the ground. Working methodically, he started snapping off the twigs from the branches and building a large pile. After watching him for several minutes, she started doing the same. When he saw that she had the hang of it, he moved on to picking up larger limbs.

It was tedious work and she could see the sweat on his face and wetting the back of his shirt.

They didn't stop until they had a pile of logs and an even bigger pile of twigs. Using a big stick, he drew a circle, maybe three feet wide, and started to dig out the dirt, making a small circular trench.

"I don't want to tell you what to do," Elle said, her tone hesitant. "But if you build the fire there, it's going to be difficult to protect the fire from the rain that will inevitably fall. If you move over there, under those heavy palms, it might be better."

Brody walked over to the area she'd indicated. "It's drier over here," he said.

She nodded.

He looked at her rather oddly. "If you have a better idea than I do, Elle, speak up. We can't afford to make any mistakes out here."

She shrugged, feeling uncomfortable. It was just that in her experience, Brody Donovan didn't make mistakes. He always seemed to have the right answer, know the right thing to do, make the right choice.

He drew another circle and started digging his two-inch-deep trench. Then he arranged four of the logs, end to end, in a pyramid style, and filled the bottom of the pyramid in with the smaller twigs.

He struck a match and, very carefully protecting it from the wind, held it in the center of the pyramid. After just a second, she could tell that the twigs had caught fire.

Tears came to her eyes and they had nothing to do with the smoke in the air.

And she was reminded of a Tom Hanks movie that she'd seen years ago. He'd been the lone survivor of a plane crash on some island, and she could vividly recall the scene where he successfully managed to get a fire going.

Fire sustained life.

And right now that felt really good.

"Thank you," she said. "This makes a difference," she said. "Somebody will find us," she added, somehow wanting him to know that she believed his earlier statement.

BRODY HEARD THE hopefulness in Elle's voice. He had learned the value of hope in the cold, mountainous terrain of Afghanistan. And the power of fire. He could have gotten a fire started without the matches, but they were definitely a plus. He counted them. Fourteen left. They would have to be careful to keep the fire going in the event that it took some time for rescuers to come.

But he wasn't going to dwell on that. He turned when his peripheral vision caught Captain Ramano in the doorway of the plane. The man stepped onto the jungle floor and studied the nose of the small plane. It was pretty much trashed, having taken a beating when they'd first skimmed the trees.

The majority of the fuselage remained intact—if anyone wasn't overly concerned about a two-foot hole in the roof. It was hard to tell if Captain Ramano was concerned or not. He barely looked at the rest of the plane before he wandered off in the jungle to take a leak.

That didn't make sense. Granted, the man had taken a jolt to the head and no doubt had a slight concussion. But even so, it was his plane.

Brody had dealt with a lot of aviators in the air force, and his friend Ethan had been a helicopter pilot in the army. Fliers were normally take-charge types.

They felt very responsible for their planes and for the individuals aboard. Brody knew that if Ethan had been flying a plane that had encountered mechanical problems, he would have been all over the wreckage, trying to figure out what had happened.

It was almost as if Captain Ramano was trying not to look at it. Which seemed odd. But one thing Brody had learned in recent years, in war-torn countries where no one escaped unscathed, was that everybody coped in his or her own way.

When the man returned to the plane, it was more of the same. He glanced at the fire, at Elle, and finally at Brody. Then he went back inside without a word.

Brody could see the questions in Elle's pretty eyes, but he ignored them. If Captain Ramano was out of the game, so be it. The plane wasn't going to fly again. His skills as a pilot were of no use to them.

Almost as soon as Captain Ramano went inside, Mr. and Mrs. Hardy came outside. Mrs. Hardy had raided her suitcase and come up with something sparkly that she spread on the ground. Then she pulled up a log near the fire that Brody had built, and both she and Mr. Hardy leaned back, him with a book, her with a deck of cards, as if the jungle had been a scheduled stop.

As if anyone regularly picnicked in a place where poisonous frogs, tarantulas and jaguars lingered nearby.

Chapter Five

Brody wanted to order the Hardys back inside, where they would have less chance of being bitten or stung by something that could seriously compromise their well-being. But he didn't say anything. If they could pretend that everything was *just fine,* then more power to them.

Elle offered the Hardys some bug repellant. Mr. Hardy took some and put it on his wife. Then Mrs. Hardy reciprocated. It was sweet.

Five minutes later, Mrs. Hardy was jawing on Mr. Hardy for breathing too loud.

Hell, maybe he ought to thank Elle from saving him from marriage. She had found a big walking stick and she was using it to poke around at various plants. She was smart to be careful. Everything in the jungle sort of blended in, and grabbing hold of a snake was guaranteed to make a bad day even worse. He watched her for about five minutes before he approached. "What are you doing?"

"The husband of the couple that I worked for in Peru was a scientist, and one of his hobbies was studying plant life in the jungle. He loved to talk about plants, to show the pictures that he would take on his jungle trips. I learned a few things while I was there. The berries on this evergreen tree are allspice. They're edible. On the other hand, this is a curare plant. Very poisonous."

He was impressed. He knew next to nothing about jungle fauna. Her knowledge might come in very handy.

"I'm not as worried about our food supply as I am our water," Elle said. "We barely have enough to last a day. But fortunately, there are multiple ways to access water in the jungle. Come here." She motioned him over to a plant with long green-and-white leaves and a brightly colored flower in the middle. It was literally growing out of the trunk of a tree. "This species is a bromeliad. The leaves overlap and when it rains, water is captured in the little pockets at the base of the flower."

He thought about what he had with him that they could use to gather water. "Probably some of us have small plastic bags in our luggage that had our liquids in them. Maybe we could use that."

"Good idea. Once it rains, which it undoubtedly will, we'll capture the water then. The other thing we can do is get water from those bamboo trees," she said, pointing off to her left, where there was a whole stand of tall, skinny bamboo plants. "It takes some patience but it's relatively easy. All we have to do is bend the bamboo stick, somehow tie it down, and cut it at the bottom. The water inside the bamboo will drain out."

"And we can drink that?"

"Yes. Probably even without boiling it. We might also find water in a nearby stream. That could be dangerous to drink if we don't boil it first. That's why I'm so darn happy to see the fire."

He studied her. He wasn't surprised at her knowledge. It was one of the things that he'd always really appreciated about Elle. She knew a little about a whole lot of things. How to make a good Hollandaise sauce. How to grow orchids in pots on their small patio. How to build a model airplane. How to dance the tango. His mother had once described her as very eclectic and she'd meant it as a compliment.

Elle had always dismissed her knowledge, saying that she knew a bunch of really useless things that were good for starting a conversation at a party but for little else. *I'm just a cocktail waitress,* she used to say.

"Should we boil all the water we gather just in case since we have a fire going?" Brody asked.

"I think so. Better safe than sorry."

"Perhaps Mrs. Hardy will want to brew herself a cup of hot tea?"

"How are your parents, Brody?" Elle asked, evidently remembering his earlier comment about his mother and tea.

"Good. Dad is still writing. Mom has cut back on her consulting and is doing quite a bit of volunteer work at their local hospital." He paused. "How's your mom?"

Elle looked startled, as if she hadn't expected the question. "I don't know. I haven't talked to her since shortly after I left the States."

She had not just walked away from him. She'd walked away from her family, too. What the hell?

"It's sort of pretty, isn't it?" she asked, changing topics quickly. "I mean, if we were here sightseeing, we'd think that."

They would. The plant and flower colors were vibrant and he'd probably already seen ten different types of birds. When he first came out of the plane earlier, there'd been a couple monkeys in the trees, cackling. Probably laughing their asses off at them.

He saw motion out of the corner of his eye

and realized that Mr. and Mrs. Hardy were already gathering up their things and heading back inside. He waited a few minutes and followed them. They'd started some kind of domino game with Pamela. Brody knelt down next to Angus. The young man was awake and definitely running a low-grade temp. The first-aid kit had not contained a thermometer, so Brody couldn't get a true reading. A low temp could be a reaction to the injury—the body giving a shout-out that hey, all is not right. Or it could mean something much worse. If that was the case, the young man needed to be in a fully equipped hospital where they could pump some antibiotics into him.

It was infuriating. He'd saved the young man's leg and he could still lose him to infection.

Captain Ramano was sitting in one of the seats, his head back, his eyes closed. His breathing was steady. Brody didn't wake him.

He stepped outside the plane, expecting to see Elle.

But there was no one there.

His heart started to beat very fast. Maybe she'd stepped away to go to the bathroom. He waited.

He didn't hear or see anything.

"Elle," he called.

No response.

"Elle!" This time he really yelled.

He heard rustling off to his left. She appeared. "What?" she asked, her tone anxious.

Relief flooded his body. And that irritated the hell out of him. "I couldn't see you," he said, sounding very much like a petulant six-year-old. "I don't want to have to go chasing after you in the jungle."

"I wanted a better view," she said. "I didn't go far. I just walked up that hill," she said, pointing to a rise about two hundred yards out. "I would not expect you to chase after me, Brody."

Oh, really? He should just let her die in the jungle? "I tried that once," he said. "You know, the chasing, and it didn't work out so well for me."

Her heard her quick inhale and knew that his verbal punch had landed. Maybe not a knock-out, but it had been a solid left hook. It should have made him happier.

Unfortunately, it made him feel like scum.

And it made him feel even worse when she didn't come back with something but rather just took the punch. As if she deserved it.

"Well?" he asked, after a very awkward moment of silence. "Were you able to see anything?"

To her credit, she didn't march off and refuse

to talk to him. Instead, she stood her ground. "Not really," she said. "It's not high enough. We probably need to get at least that high," she said, pointing to her right. Off in the distance, he couldn't tell how far, was higher ground. Having grown up in the Colorado mountains, in Crow Hollow, Brody couldn't call it a mountain. At best, a small foothill. But she was right. It would probably give them a good view in every direction.

Getting there would be a bitch. Walking in the jungle wasn't like walking on the treadmill at the gym.

"What do you think?" she asked.

"About what?"

"About next steps," she pushed.

Even though he'd known better than to hope for a rescue plane last night, he'd still spent the night listening for engine sounds. He'd been doing the same this morning. Unfortunately, he'd heard nothing like that. He was just about to give her some glib reassurance, but he saw the look in her eyes. The message in them was clear. *Be real, Brody.*

"I don't know what to think," he said. "If Angus's distress call went through, somebody should be out looking for us. I know the Amazon is huge, but they don't have to search all of it. How tough is it to identify the potential area where the plane crashed? They hear the call, they look at their radar, and somebody ought to be smart enough to figure out where our particular blip fell off the screen."

"Maybe the distress call never went through?"

"Even so, air-traffic control should have been tracking us. I assume there is some regular communication between them and a pilot. When Captain Ramano didn't answer, that should have made somebody sit up straighter in their chair. Even if that didn't happen, somebody surely noticed when our plane didn't land as expected. It's been light for several hours. What's taking them so long?"

"I guess that gets back to the sheer magnitude of the jungle. Even with some idea of where we are, it's probably like looking for the needle in the proverbial haystack."

He nodded. "Then we have to hope for the best."

"So we wait?" she asked.

"For now," he said. "But I think we should start to gather and boil water. Just in case."

"What are we going to boil it in?"

"I think we can use the first-aid kit. It's probably twelve inches by eight inches and several inches deep. I'm going to build a grate to go over the open fire."

"I'll gather up things that we can use to collect the water in," she said.

He nodded. It was good to have someone else in the group to count on. Pamela didn't seem all that steady. Mr. and Mrs. Hardy were too elderly and Angus was out of the race. Captain Ramano was the unknown. So far, he'd been distant, not even intellectually curious about their predicament. The one good thing was that he wasn't complaining about pain anywhere except his head, which was a good sign that he'd managed to escape internal injuries.

If Brody and Elle could remain civil to each other, they had a chance of making it out of here. So far, she'd shown amazing strength. She'd been calm, resilient and had come up with good solutions.

Of the two of them, he'd been the bigger ass. It wasn't something to be terribly proud of.

TWO HOURS LATER, Elle sat inside the plane, looking out one of the small windows. The rain had come, forcing them all inside.

Just as it dampened the earth, it seemed to dampen everyone's spirits. No one was talking. Not even Mrs. Hardy.

And the silence gave Elle plenty of opportunity to think.

She'd been so stupid earlier when she asked

about his parents. But she'd really liked Mr. and Mrs. Donovan. They were super nice to her and always made her feel welcome in their home. They were so smart, so successful, yet they treated her as an equal.

She'd honestly been curious about them, but she'd never have asked if she'd thought that that would prompt Brody to ask about her mother. Brody had never met her mom. She didn't figure he lost much sleep thinking about it.

If he'd been startled by her announcement that she hadn't spoken to her mother for thirteen years, he'd hidden it well. For only a second, she'd again debated lying and saying something innocuous, such as she's fine. But the truth had popped out.

She was done lying and especially done with lying to Brody Donovan. She didn't have any reason to tell him the whole ugly truth; nothing would be gained by that. But she wasn't going to compound her errors and continue her lies.

When they had been dating, Elle was able to explain away Catherine Rivers's absence from her life. Whenever Brody had asked about her family, she'd made up some crazy excuse about her mom living in Utah and not liking to fly.

She had no idea whether her mother liked to fly. They'd never discussed it during their brief telephone conversations that occurred two or three times a year, whenever Elle forced herself to dial the damn phone and endure the stilted, forced exchange that passed as mother-daughter bonding.

After they became engaged, Brody had insisted that he needed to meet her mother, to officially ask for permission to marry Elle. He said that he did not want their first meeting to be at the wedding.

How could she tell Brody that she hadn't planned on inviting Catherine to the wedding? It would have spurred all kinds of questions that she didn't want to answer, didn't plan on ever answering.

Elle had tried to convince him that it wasn't necessary to ask permission, that she'd talked to her mom and the woman was on board. But Brody had worked like crazy to arrange a couple days off and had purchased two round-trip tickets from Boston to Salt Lake City. She'd left the country four days before the trip was to occur.

And to this day, had very little contact with Catherine.

The conversation about parents had left her shaken. After Brody had gone back inside the plane, she'd had to do something to expel the anxiety that had flooded her system with the mention of her mother.

Sure, she'd wanted a better view, but what she'd really needed was a little space, a little time to compartmentalize her thoughts about Catherine. She'd practically run up the small hill and, once there, had stood at the rise, her breath coming hard. By the time he'd come back outside and had been yelling for her, she was back in control.

So he didn't want to have to chase after her.

She didn't want him to. Had never wanted that. Had hoped he wouldn't and had made it as difficult as she could if he actually tried.

She'd had to. She hadn't been sure that she was strong enough to walk away a second time.

Now, as they all huddled in the aircraft and listened to the afternoon rain hit the outside of the plane, she covertly watched Brody. He was looking out one of the small windows. She knew he was worried about the fire.

She thought it would likely be okay. He'd built a grate out of bamboo that traversed the circumference of the fire circle and then had hung the wire hanger of the first-aid kit over one of the long bamboo sticks. The first-aid kit swung freely over the fire and they'd successfully managed to boil a small amount of water and saved it in one of the empty water bottles.

He'd also constructed, over the fire, a crude-looking tepee that was about four feet high at the apex. He'd covered the sides with thick palm leaves, giving the fire even more protection.

Mrs. Hardy had looked at it on one of her trips outside and proclaimed him a genius. Elle knew that there were more matches and it would be possible to start another fire. It dawned on her that Brody was already preparing for the worst—for the likelihood that it might be many days before they were found.

The downpour lasted about forty minutes. When it was over, Elle put on her water shoes. She didn't intend to go wading through any standing water, but the ground would be damp and she wanted to keep her loafers as dry as possible. She motioned to Pamela and then to Mrs. Hardy, who had earlier insisted that she was able to help collect water.

They followed her outside, as did Brody. She showed them how to gather water from the plants. Once Elle explained that they needed to gather water so that it could be boiled, Pamela had run back to the plane and come out again minutes later, holding what appeared to be a ball of tissue paper. She'd peeled back the paper to reveal a brightly colored coffee cup.

"I bought this in Brasília for my nephew. We can use it to collect water."

"It's beautiful," Elle said. "But we need to be

careful to keep dirty and clean utensils separate. Let's make sure that no water goes into that cup that hasn't been boiled. Then we can all drink from it. We'll gather the water in these plastic bags."

"We can also use my coffeepot," Mrs. Hardy said.

Brody, Elle, and Pamela had immediately stopped what they were doing. "You have a coffeepot in your suitcase?" Elle asked.

"Never travel without it. It's just a little four-cupper."

Brody shook his head. "Mrs. Hardy, you don't happen to have a spare plane in your luggage, do you?"

"Why, no, I don't," she said. "But I may put it on the list for the next trip."

The other three exchanged looks. Elle knew what she was thinking and suspected the others were tracking. She hoped Mrs. Hardy got to take another trip. She hoped they all did.

"It's good to know we have another vessel to use," Elle said. "We'll use it to brew tea."

"Now you're talking," Mrs. Hardy said, and got busy gathering water. With multiple trips to the first-aid kit with their baggies, Pamela and Mrs. Hardy were able to fill the container with water in less than forty minutes. While they did that, Elle gathered edible berries in a basket that she fashioned out of one of Mr. Hardy's long-sleeved shirts. She found several coconuts, as well.

"It's a tropical feast tonight," she said, bringing her stash back to the group.

Mrs. Hardy smiled. Pamela rolled her eyes, but she did give the coconuts an appreciative glance. Elle looked for Mrs. Hardy's knife to cut the coconuts and realized that Brody was using it to notch out a couple long sticks. Elle wasn't sure what he was doing until she saw him use the sticks to hook the handle of the first-aid kit after the water had boiled for ten minutes.

Mrs. Hardy was right. He was pretty damn smart. If someone had tried to grab the handle, it would have been so hot that they'd have likely jerked back and risked dumping all the freshly boiled water.

"Whatcha got?" he asked, catching her eye.

"Coconuts. Young ones that will have more milk. Mature ones that will have good meat inside."

At her school, Father Taquero used a hammer and a nail to drill a hole through the coconut so that the sweet milk would drain out. She didn't have a nail or a hammer, but she did have sharp eyebrow tweezers and a flat piece of wood to hit them with.

She got her tools and they worked as intended. She held the coconut over Pamela's cup and the watery milk drained out. She held it up toward Pamela. "You first. You're the one who had the cup."

Pamela took a tentative sip. She pulled back. "That's good," she said.

"And full of things that are good for you," Elle said. "You know people have survived a very long time with just coconuts."

"I hope we don't have to do that," Pamela said, her voice low. "Can I ask you something?" she added.

"Of course."

"You knew Dr. Donovan before this, didn't you?"

Had Mrs. Hardy said something? She didn't think so. Unfortunately, Pamela had definitely heard Brody's first comment, too. "I did," she admitted. "We knew each other many years ago but haven't seen each other for more than a decade."

"I think you were more than casual friends."

Had Brody said something? "Why?" Elle asked.

"Because of the way he looks at you when you're not looking."

And damn her needy self, because she wanted to know more. "I'm sure it's nothing," she said, dismissing the comment and turning away before Pamela could see the warmth flood her face.

Chapter Six

By evening, Mrs. Hardy's internal battery had evidently recharged and she was talking like crazy, telling a very long story about some friends who'd been on a cruise ship that had mechanical trouble and the deplorable conditions that they'd had to endure until help came some five days later. At one point, when she was providing intimate details of one woman's conversation with the ship's purser, she said, "Well, you know Delores."

Pamela stood up suddenly. "No. No, I don't know Delores and I don't know any of these other stupid people that you're talking about and even more important, I don't care. Just please shut up."

Mrs. Hardy's already wrinkled face crumpled and her eyes filled with tears.

Mr. Hardy shot an evil stare at Pamela but didn't say anything. He just patted his wife's hand.

"Bitch," Captain Ramano said, almost under his breath.

Pamela turned on him. "This is your fault," she yelled. "You and your shoddy little plane's fault."

Elle sucked in a breath, waiting for Captain Ramano to reveal exactly whose fault it really was. But the man simply leaned his head back and closed his eyes.

"You don't know what you're talking about, lady," Angus said, anxious to protect his friend. "You're alive because of Captain Ramano."

Pamela whirled toward him. "We never should have been flying in that storm. I'm going to sue everyone involved. Every single person."

Elle stood up. "Listen," she said. "We're all under a lot of stress. It's easy to say or do things that probably aren't in our best interest right now. We can't let the situation get to us. We need each other. And we're going to have to work at getting along in order to survive this."

Pamela muttered something and Elle stared at her. Finally, Pamela waved a hand. "Fine," she said. "I'm sorry," she added to no one in particular.

For the moment, the tension appeared abated. Elle had done a good job, Brody thought, but it was only a matter of time before frustration mounted again. As the hours dragged on, even the most levelheaded would react to the strain.

He'd been so confident that they would be rescued today. Probably had been blindly optimistic in his approach. This was no *Field of Dreams*. He could build all the fires he wanted and still they might not come.

They were going to have to do more than simply wait. And for the past hour, an idea had been kicking around in his head. He would go for help. It was really the only answer.

He walked outside to add more wood to the fire. Between him and Elle, they had gathered enough wood during the day to keep the fire going for days. Food would be gone within a day, but thanks to Elle's help, there would be water. Maybe not a lot but certainly enough to sustain life. Plus there was fruit, thanks to Elle helping them identify what they could and could not eat.

They couldn't wait forever for someone to find the wreckage. He'd been a Boy Scout. Hell, a damn Eagle Scout. He knew how to tell directions by the sun and how to mark a trail so that he could lead someone back for the others.

He would leave at first light.

He heard a noise behind him. It was Elle. She came up and stood next to him at the fire.

That surprised him. For most of the day, unless there was a need to communicate, they'd kept their distance from each other. Now neither of them said anything for a minute. Finally, she turned to him.

"I'm going to go for help," she said.

No. That had been his line. "That's crazy," he said.

Her spine straightened. "Pardon me," she said, her tone icy.

Was he doomed to always say the wrong thing around her? Maybe it was because she raised emotion in him that interfered with what was usually a consistent ability to moderate his comments and actions. "If anyone is going to go for help, it's going to be me," he said.

"Why?"

Because you're a girl clearly wasn't the right answer. It wasn't because he considered women to be the weaker sex. He was pretty sure that the women he served with were smarter and worked harder than most of his male counterparts. And physically, Elle was clearly in good shape and could probably handle the terrain.

But the jungle was full of danger. From all venues. Poisonous plants. Carnivorous animals. And when he'd been researching the area prior to his trip, he learned that the jungle was still home to a number of humans who might not necessarily be friendly.

Elle could be injured, attacked, even killed.

He would never forgive himself.

"Because I already made the decision that I'm going," he said, knowing it was a lame excuse.

"You don't know the jungle. I do."

"You're needed here. You're the voice of reason. You can keep everybody calmed down."

"There are injured here. You're the only one who has the skills to treat them."

"I can't do anything else for either Angus or Captain Ramano. And I'm afraid that time is not Angus's friend. I'm confident that he's developing an infection. Every hour he goes without an antibiotic is an hour closer to losing that leg or even his life. I have to go and I have to go soon."

"What's your plan?" she asked.

He shrugged. "Walk until I find help."

"Which direction?" she prodded.

"North. We're south of the Amazon River. If I can get there, we have a good likelihood that there will be someone who can help us."

"It's too far. It would take you weeks to walk that distance."

She was probably right. But it had seemed

like the best option. "Then I guess I'll head south, back toward Brasília."

She shook her head. "We flew for about twenty minutes before we crashed. I asked Angus how fast we were flying and he said about 250 knots or roughly 300 miles per hour. Our destination was north, at about a thirty-degree angle. I think we're roughly 130 miles north and just a little east of Brasília. If I'm right, that means we're less than a two-day walk to Mantau. It's a small village, due east, and I have a friend there who can help us. That's why I'm the one who is leaving at first light."

Her math made sense. Her confidence was admirable.

And her stubbornness was damn irritating. "But—"

"Brody," she said, her voice softer. "You have always wanted to take care of things for everybody else. I suspect that makes you a great doctor. You care. But you don't have to shoulder this burden alone. I can do it."

He stared at her. So beautiful in the firelight. So determined to convince him that she was right. He could not let her go by herself. There was really only one solution.

It didn't appeal to him as a particularly great one. "We'll go together," he said.

She stared at him.

And he thought for a moment that she might back down, that the idea of traipsing through the jungle, just the two of them, was enough to make her rethink her strategy. Thus far, they'd managed to coexist. But he could feel the energy swirling just below the surface and thought it was unlikely that she was oblivious of it. Like hot lava bubbling up through the cracks, there were buried emotions waiting to spew out, to scratch and rip at old scars that had taken forever to heal.

"Do you think that's wise?" she asked finally.

"Hell, no," he said.

He thought he caught a flicker of hurt in her pretty eyes but he couldn't be sure. Maybe it was just the reflection of the fire.

"We'll leave at first light," she said.

"Fine," he replied, gritting his teeth.

She turned and walked away without another word. He stood by the fire and listened to the sounds of the jungle. There were chirps and caws and the subtle rustle of leaves. And it was not a stretch to imagine that there were eyes watching him.

After several minutes he went back inside the plane. It was becoming an oppressively small space and the smell of damp air and human fear and frustration permeated it.

Mrs. Hardy was digging around in her ruined suitcase. She pulled out an envelope. When she opened the flap, there were dozens of snapshots inside.

"What are those?" Pamela asked, evidently trying to make amends.

"Pictures of my grandchildren," Mrs. Hardy said. "I have seven of them. Ages three to seventeen." She handed a photo to Pamela. "That's all of us last Christmas."

"Very nice," Pamela said.

"Do you have children?" Mrs. Hardy asked.

Pamela frowned. "I have a very important job and I work sixty hours a week. I don't have time for children."

"Of course," Mrs. Hardy said, nodding. "How about you, Captain Ramano? Any children or grandchildren?"

"Two sons," the man said. "Both married in the last couple of years but no grandchildren yet. You and Mr. Hardy are very fortunate."

Given that the captain had been mostly uncommunicative, Brody was surprised that he'd tacked on the last sentiment. He prepared himself for the inevitable question given that Mrs. Hardy seemed determined to work her way around the small space. *No wife, no children.*

Four words. That's all he had to say. Didn't have to offer up any excuses, as Pamela had felt inclined to do. Certainly wasn't going to admit that on more than one occasion he'd thought about how different his life might be if he and Elle had gotten married. They might have a houseful of kids by now.

That would be nice. He'd been an only child growing up and had wished for siblings. Maybe that was why Ethan and Mack had been so important. Brothers. Just not the same bloodline.

Mrs. Hardy turned to Elle. "What about you, dear? Do you have children?"

He thought Elle hesitated just a moment too long. Then she offered up a sad smile. "I do. Mia. She's eleven."

Brody could feel the blood rush to his head. She had a child?

She'd said she never married.

Yet she'd loved some man enough to carry his child.

"Do you have a picture of her?" Mrs. Hardy asked.

His head was buzzing so loud that he didn't hear Elle's response. But she pulled her phone out of her backpack and turned it on. Within seconds she was handing it to Mrs. Hardy.

"Oh, she's lovely," Mrs. Hardy said.

"Thank you," Elle said. "She's very sweet."

Mrs. Hardy gave the phone to her husband, who nodded appropriately and then, at Mrs. Hardy's urging, handed the phone to Pamela.

And Brody had to practically sit on his damn hands to keep from reaching out. Why the hell did he care? She had a child. What difference did it make?

He didn't know. But it did.

Eleven? She certainly hadn't wasted any time.

"Almost a teenager," Pamela said, when she looked at the phone. "They say those are the toughest years."

Elle smiled and her eyes filled with tears. "She can hardly wait to be thirteen. It's all she talks about. She's frustrated that she has to be twelve first."

Pamela handed the phone to Captain Ramano. He looked at it, then at Elle. "She go to that school you teach at?" he asked.

It was odd but Brody thought Elle's chin jerked up, as if the question had surprised her. She nodded. "Yes, she does."

Brody couldn't stand another minute. He got up, opened the plane door and walked outside into the dark night.

Had she not loved the father enough to marry him? Had she left him, too?

Had he not wanted her or the child?

Idiot.

Hell. His thoughts were bouncing around, making his head ache. He walked over and stood next to the fire that he'd fed all day and would feed again several times during the night.

The smoke burned his eyes.

Off in the distance, he heard the howl of something wild. He felt a bit like making the same noise.

He'd spent years missing her like crazy and she'd been humming along, living life to the fullest. Meeting a guy. Having his baby.

Suddenly it was May 10 and he was standing by the mailbox in his bare feet all over again. The pain was intense.

When she told him that she'd never married, he'd told himself it didn't matter one way or the other. He was over her. Had been over her for a long time.

Even though he'd been assigned to a military post in the Middle East for long stretches, he'd also been stateside a number of times over the years. Colleagues and family friends had fixed him up. The women had been nice.

He'd even slept with a couple of them.

He was over her.

But that didn't stop him from knowing that there was a big difference between having a physical relationship with somebody, which was really just biology, and having the connection of a child.

She might not have married but she'd committed herself in an even more important way. To someone else.

His gut hurt and it wasn't from eating fresh coconut.

When the hell was he going to stop being stupid over Elle Vollman?

Chapter Seven

Elle thought she was the first one awake the next morning. The inside of the plane was dark. She turned on her flashlight. She could see the Hardys. Mr. Hardy had his head on Mrs. Hardy's shoulder. Elle could hear Pamela and Captain Ramano. They were both snoring. She turned in her seat so that she could see Angus. His eyes were closed but his breathing seemed shallow. He'd thrown off his blanket and it appeared he was sweating.

Brody was likely right. Angus was on the decline.

She flashed her light in the seat where Brody had slept the previous night. Empty.

He'd beaten her up. Even though she'd been asleep before he came back inside the plane the night before.

She guessed it wasn't her business if he was tired today. It was too bad they didn't have any coffee for Mrs. Hardy's pot. It was really too bad that they didn't have any electricity to plug it in. It was really, really too bad that she couldn't have her favorite barista at the local coffee shop whip up a nonfat latte with a shot of hazelnut.

"One little cup of coffee," she whispered, as she pulled on socks. "That's all I'm asking for." She slipped her shoes on. "And maybe a cherry-walnut scone. Warm," she added because if she was going to dream, she might as well dream big.

"That sounds lovely, dear," Mrs. Hardy whispered back in the dark. "Don't forget the butter. And I do love a bit of cream in my coffee."

Elle flashed her light in the older woman's direction. "I didn't realize you were awake," she said.

"Just for a few minutes. I'm worried about you and Dr. Donovan. Don't you think you can just wait for someone to rescue us? I mean, we have some food and water, thanks to you. Do you really have to go traipsing off in the jungle?"

Elle knew their grip on survival was tenuous at best. And to sit back and wait wasn't her nature. Plus, she had this crazy feeling that danger was close. Didn't know where the danger was coming from, but her gut was telling her that time was of the essence.

She'd tried to push away her crazy thoughts that somehow T. K. Jamas was responsible for the crash and that he wouldn't rest until he knew that he'd succeeded in keeping her from testifying. When Captain Ramano had asked whether Mia attended the school where she taught, it had startled her. She didn't recall ever telling Captain Ramano that she was a teacher. How did he know? It had been the middle of the night when she explained to Brody about the books and her teaching position. Captain Ramano had been sleeping. She supposed it was possible that he'd simply been pretending to be asleep and had been listening to everything around him, but she didn't think so.

How had he known about her school? Why had he known that?

Surely, he could not have been in cahoots with T. K. Jamas. No pilot would deliberately crash his own plane? Unless he was desperate.

And T. K. Jamas made people desperate. In a corner, getting poked with a sharp stick kind of desperate.

And evidently he also made them tongue-tied. If Captain Ramano knew why his plane had suddenly developed mechanical trouble, he wasn't talking.

Going for help was the only answer. And if that meant that she had to endure another couple days of Brody's snide remarks, so be it. She deserved them. She deserved worse.

"We'll be fine," she said. "By tomorrow night, we should be able to make contact with my friend and send help to you."

"At least if you get injured, Dr. Donovan will be able to take care of you," Mrs. Hardy said.

She wasn't so sure. If she tripped and fell, he'd likely be inclined to just leave her in the jungle to die. The Hippocratic oath *might* save her—he was always a stickler for playing by the rules.

There weren't really any rules in the jungle. While she brushed her hair, she amused herself with thinking about jungle rules. Rule number 1: Run fast when being chased by a lion. Rule number 2: Never sit on anything that moves. Rule number 3: Avoid alligators at all cost.

She could go on and on, but while it was a fun little mind game, these were very real threats. She could only hope that she and Brody had good luck.

She was determined that he wasn't going to regret her insistence to come along. She opened her backpack and checked the contents. Once she'd decided to walk for help, she'd examined the contents of her small carry-on bag. She had very little with her because she'd been intending to purchase something to wear once she got back to the States. Her wardrobe needs at her small school were pretty basic, just pants and a shirt. Certainly not appropriate for a meeting with government officials.

Although she suspected what she wore was of considerable less importance to them than what she was going to say.

Human trafficking.

Young girls sold into a dank underworld of sick, twisted souls who used and abused them until they finally put them out of their misery and killed them.

Big business. And she'd trusted the person who was at the top of the pyramid. Had inadvertently helped him find innocent girls to prey upon. That still made her sick.

But he would pay. Her testimony would ensure that. She could still recall the excitement in the agent's voice when she'd told him why she was calling and what she knew.

Evidently, T. K. Jamas had been on their radar screen for years, but they had no hard evidence to charge and convict him.

Until now.

She just had to find her way out of the jungle first.

Last night, after she'd verified that she hadn't packed any socks, she immediately went to Pamela and explained what she needed. The woman had opened her suitcase and there were two pairs, besides the pair on her feet. She'd given both to Elle. "Take whatever you need. Just find somebody who can help us," she'd said.

Elle had assured her that they would and had finished packing her backpack. She kept it light, adding a change of clothing, her flashlight and her cell phone, just in case. She had kept one of the tubes of bug repellant and left the other with Mrs. Hardy to dole out as needed to those they were leaving behind.

Initially, Elle had assumed that she and Brody would take some water with them but leave the food behind. Mrs. Hardy had claimed that she wouldn't be able to sleep knowing that Elle and Brody were doing the difficult work of traipsing through the jungle without food. Finally, Elle had agreed that she and Brody would take one breakfast bar and some nuts along with enough water to get them to their first campsite. She'd added that to her backpack. Then, at Mrs. Hardy's insistence, she'd added the coffeepot. It made sense. They would need something to boil water in.

Mrs. Hardy had also assured her that she and Pamela would take care of getting more water from the bamboo stalks. Elle knew she couldn't count on Angus to do much—he had to keep his leg immobilized. And Captain Ramano mostly slept. He did wake up long enough to say that he'd watch over the fire. They left one of the matchbooks with him just in case it was extinguished by rain and needed to be rebuilt.

If her calculations were correct, and if their walk through the jungle went well, they could be in Mantau by tomorrow night, sitting at Leo Arroul's table. And there was no doubt that Leo would help. She'd first met the man almost five years before, even before coming to Brazil. He was a friend of friends, originally from Canada, but had been living in Brazil for years when they'd ended up at the same dinner party in Peru. He'd told her about Father Taquero and his school for girls and years later, when she'd been looking for someplace to settle down, someplace where she could make a difference, she'd thought of the school.

Leo had made his money in the stock market and after his wife of twenty-two years had left him for her personal trainer, he'd left his job, left his country, and for the last ten years, had dedicated his life to helping purify water systems in the jungle. He was a person who knew how to get things done.

She heard a noise behind her and turned. Brody was coming back inside the plane, dressed in the same jeans as yesterday with a different long-sleeved shirt. He had on his boots again, with his pant legs tucked it. He had his duffel bag over one shoulder.

She waited for him to say good morning. He didn't.

She pointed to the many red fabric scraps that were tied up and down on the bag's strap. "Nice decoration."

He shrugged. "My favorite red shirt. It makes sense to mark a trail."

Of course it did. But he'd said it as if he was looking for an argument.

It was going to be a long couple of days.

He opened his bag. Inside was his water bottle, some clothing and the remains of the parachute. "What are you bringing that for?" she asked. It had to weigh several pounds, and over many miles, that added up to a whole lot of strain on a shoulder.

"I'm hoping I can find two trees, tie an end up to each one, and make a hammock."

It was a good idea. Sleeping outside in the jungle was a horrifying thought, and having to sleep on the ground in the jungle took it up a notch. She'd put the remaining newspaper in her backpack along with a blanket, figuring that she'd put the newspaper on the ground, wrap the blanket around her as tight as possible and sleep sitting up. It wasn't perfect but it was the best she'd been able to come up with.

"You may want to take a blanket, too," she said.

He shook his head. "That would only leave them with two for five people. I'll be fine. Let's go. We're going to need to find more water along the way."

"We will," she said. "Look for ants. Trails of them. They can lead you to a water source."

He stared at her. "You're certainly full of jungle folklore."

Was he trying to pick a fight? "I've lived in Brazil for several years. I do know a couple things. If you can stand the idea of taking advice from me, you might actually learn a couple things."

He stared at her and she could hear him suck in a deep breath. "I've learned, Elle. Trust me on this one. You taught me several important life lessons."

And he would never forgive her. "This is a mistake," she said. "I'm going by myself." She turned on her heel.

"No," he said. He moved fast and got in front of her. "Look, I'm sorry. Let's just get going. We can do this. I can do this."

Above the ringing in her ears, she could hear the squawk of birds and the squeal of nearby monkeys. "Fine," she said, her teeth jammed together so tight she was surprised she didn't crack one.

Brody nodded, looking relieved. "I've got Mrs. Hardy's knife and a few basic medical supplies. And I have one of the small plastic bags for the matches. Above all else, we need to try to keep them dry."

He zipped his duffel and slung the strap over his head so that the strap crossed his torso and the bag rested at his hip. It left both of his hands free.

"Here's the bug stuff," she said. "We'll take one tube with us and leave the other one for the rest of the group." She walked toward the plane and picked up the two walking sticks that she'd hunted for earlier. She handed the taller one to him.

"Thank you," he mumbled. He pointed at the cut on her forehead. She'd taken off the bandage before she went to sleep. "Did you put more antibiotic ointment on that?"

"No. It's healing."

"Yeah. But you need to be careful." He opened his bag and pulled out a tube of the ointment. Then he put a dab on the end of his finger and smeared it over the cut. Then he got out a fresh bandage and put it on.

Damn him. It was hard to be mad at some-

body who was hell-bent on taking care of you.
Even if he didn't like you.

THEY SAID THEIR goodbyes to those remaining
behind. Mrs. Hardy hugged her hard and Mr.
Hardy patted her shoulder. Pamela voiced the
collective concern. "Don't get lost."

"We won't," she promised, praying it was
true. Following the sun was rudimentary at
best, especially in a jungle where walking in
a straight line was virtually impossible.

"Which direction are you going?" Captain
Ramano asked.

"Toward…Brasília," she said.

Brody looked at her oddly, but thankfully he
didn't say anything until they were safely away
from the plane. "Change of plans?" he asked.

"No."

They walked another hundred yards before he spoke again. "So why lie to Captain
Ramano?"

She couldn't tell him the truth. The whole
truth. "His attitude since the crash has been
bothering me."

Brody nodded. "I thought maybe it was just
me."

"No. Not you. Let's get walking."

They walked steadily for an hour, him in the
lead, her following three steps behind. His legs

were longer and she knew that he was moderating his stride so that she could keep up. Every hundred yards or so, he stopped to tie a rag onto a bush or a small tree. As she'd suspected, there was no such thing as following the trail in a straight line. There was no trail and the random nature of the plant life had them weaving back and forth. That was really the only choice. While they had Mrs. Hardy's knife, and that was certainly better than nothing, it was no match against the dense growth. That called for a machete. Every time they angled their path, she watched him lift his face and judge the direction by the morning sun that at times, was barely visible through the thick canopy of trees. She'd told him to head due east and he was doing his very best.

It was warm and getting warmer. Sweat trickled down her back and between her breasts, making her camisole damp and the cotton shirt that covered it stick to her skin. Her loafers were damp from the wet ground. Her socks were still mostly dry, but she knew that was only temporary. It was a foregone conclusion that they would get caught in one of the many rain showers that occurred on a daily basis or that they'd have to cross a body of water at some point.

That scared her the most. The idea of moving

through water that might be filled with snakes and all kinds of other dangerous things was so frightening that it was all she could think about.

There were birds everywhere, squawking and swooping, their colors brilliant against the deep green foliage. She could name a few. There were the scarlet macaws, so easily recognized with their red bodies and stripes of yellow and blue on their tail feathers. The black oropendola with its bright yellow beak and tail feathers. She'd heard its raspy call before she'd seen it.

There were so many more that she'd probably seen before but couldn't name and many that she was probably seeing for the first time. Bird enthusiasts flocked to the Amazon to see the many species.

She should probably be more appreciative.

It was hard to remember that when she had to swat at something that grazed her chin. Even with the repellent on, the bugs found her. They were everywhere. All a nuisance. Most harmless. Some likely more dangerous.

After another half hour, Brody stopped. He turned, wiping his forehead with his sleeve. "Doing okay?" he asked.

Her legs hurt, she had sweat in places that polite women didn't talk about, and she was still thinking about the coffee that she hadn't had. "Dandy," she said. "You?"

"About the same. I think we're still pretty much on course."

"I think so, too." She pulled her water bottle out of her backpack and took a drink, careful not to overindulge. "I'm guessing that even with all the twists and turns, we're still doing a twelve-or thirteen-minute mile."

"I'd say so. That's good," he added.

Once again, he was being positive, trying to keep her focused on what was going well. It was his nature. He'd been like that in med school. Even when he was bone tired and he still had three hours of homework to do, he'd been able to find something positive in the situation. If they went to a restaurant and the food was bad, he'd focus in on the drinks that were good. If they went to a movie that was bad, the popcorn and soda were just what he'd been craving. He wasn't stupid about it—and he wasn't over-the-top with it—but he simply chose to try to find something positive in every experience.

She often wondered what he'd found positive in her leaving.

"Ready?" he asked.

She put away her water bottle. "As ever," she said.

And things went pretty well for the next half hour until Brody stopped so fast that she literally ran into his back.

He turned fast, grabbed Elle's arms and steadied her, keeping her from bouncing backward and him from tumbling into what looked to be a fifty-foot-deep ravine.

"Oh, hell," Elle said, looking around him.

Indeed. The gorge was impressive—deep and stretching as far as he could see in both directions. Going around it wasn't an option.

"What do you think?" he asked.

"I'm not sure that going down is going to be any easier than going up," she said. "But we have to get across. And," she added, putting her hand up to shade her eyes from the stream of sun that managed to sneak through the canopy of trees, "that may be water." She pointed deep into the ravine.

Brody looked. The plant growth was heavy in the bottom and he couldn't be sure. It would be wonderful if it was water. They'd both been careful with their supply, but they needed more.

"I'll go first," Brody said.

He got about ten feet and looked back. Elle had shifted over at least three feet and was taking her first step.

"Is that a better path?" he asked.

"No. About the same."

"I'd prefer it if you'd stay behind me."

"That's what I was trying to avoid," she said. "Just keep going and don't worry about me."

Right. As if that was going to happen. He knew what she was doing. She was afraid that she was going to slip and if she did, she'd tumble into him and they both might end up rolling down the damn hill. But if she slipped now, she'd roll past him and he wouldn't have a chance in hell of catching her.

"Stay behind me," he said. "In the same path."

She looked as if she wanted to argue.

"Please," he said.

She rolled her eyes but then stepped diagonally, once again lining up with him.

"Thank you," he said. It was slow going and he knew that if he and Elle were both not in good shape, they would simply have not been able to do it.

By the time they got to the flat portion of the ravine, they were both panting. If it had been that much work getting down, going up would be a real bitch. "Well, that was fun," he said, not expecting an answer. But Elle had been right. He could hear water. He walked twenty feet to his right and, sure enough, behind a big, sprawling palm tree, water was trickling over a shelf of rock that jutted out from the canyon wall.

He turned to tell her. She was half bent over, her hands on her thighs, absolutely motionless.

"Elle," he said.

"Yes," she responded, her voice small.

"What's wrong?" he asked, taking big steps toward her.

"Stop," she said. "Don't come any closer. Snake."

Chapter Eight

He looked. Sure enough. Winding through the long grass, its color blending in with nature so that it was difficult to immediately discern, was a snake, almost six feet long, with slightly pink skin that was heavily dotted with brown squares.

"I think it's a bushmaster," she said.

Brody really wished he'd read his guidebook a little more closely. He tried to visualize the chapter on deadly threats. Yes. Bushmaster had been in there. Definitely poisonous.

Normally not a snake to attack, it would when provoked.

Elle had clearly provoked it by almost stepping on it. It wound around, near her feet, its head less than six inches away from her ankles.

Pamela's socks were going to be of little assistance.

"Don't move," he said.

"Can't," she whispered.

If she got bit, he would not be able to save her. The venom would travel through her bloodstream and within minutes would begin to paralyze vital organs.

He would lose her again.

Once again, a machete would have really come in handy. Or a rope that he could swing from a tree and she could catch it and be whisked away from danger.

Here, we have to use what we have.

How many times had he heard that from his commanding officer these past several years? Even when he did surgery at a fully equipped base camp, it wasn't like a North American operating room in a multimillion-dollar surgical suite. And those times when he'd had to go even closer to the front line, to administer aid to the most critically wounded, he'd performed miracles with even less.

What did he have? Mrs. Hardy's knife. And steady hands. A surgeon's hands. Used to making very accurate, precise incisions. Used to the feel of resistant flesh. Spurting blood from severed arteries was an everyday occurrence.

He pulled the knife from his pocket. Unfolded the blade.

He took another step forward, wishing for some of the steadiness to seep into his legs.

"No closer," Elle whispered. "Go. One of us has to get out of here."

Did she really think that he would just walk away, leave her at the mercy of the snake who might or might not get bored and slink away at some point? Assuming Elle could stay absolutely motionless for some prolonged period of time.

Still four feet away from Elle and the snake, he stepped sideways. Then again. One more step. He was at a ninety-degree angle. Then a cautious step toward Elle. Toward the snake.

One more.

Less than three feet separated him from Elle and the snake that now had stopped moving. Did that mean it was getting ready to strike? Damn it. He knew next to nothing about snakes.

He did, however, know something about human anatomy. And the weight of organs. And how much force it took to cut through that organ with a supersharp instrument.

By his best comparative guess, he figured the snake weighed between five and ten pounds. And Mrs. Hardy's knife was sharp but not razor sharp.

"Stay still," he said. "No matter what until I cut the snake. Then step back fast."

"Okay," she said, her voice stronger now, as if she'd managed to overcome her initial fear.

He took another step forward, close enough now that he could reach the snake. And in one smooth, fast movement, he raised his arm, squatted, and made a clean slice through the snake, separating the upper one-third of its body from the lower two-thirds.

And there was blood and twitching and slithering that seemed to go on forever. Of course, by that time, he and Elle were a safe six feet away.

He circled around the still-moving carcass and wrapped an arm around Elle, who looked as if she was about to fall down. He pulled her in close to his body. She was shaking.

"It's okay," he said. "We're both fine. The snake is dead."

"I can't look," she said.

He pulled her in tighter. "You don't have to," he said, his mouth close to her ear.

"I guess it's just another average day in the jungle," she said, her face still against his chest.

He smiled and, without thinking, bent his head and kissed her forehead. She stilled. Then raised her face.

"Brody," she whispered.

She was so beautiful. And he could not help himself.

He bent his head and kissed her. And it was if the thirteen years apart had never happened.

This was Elle. He knew her lips. Knew the feel of her teeth against his tongue. Knew the little sounds she made.

And he might have kissed her forever if the wild screech of a low-flying bird had not had them jumping back from each other.

"Oh," Elle said, her fingers touching her lips.

Hell. Now his legs felt really weak. He tried to summon the memory that it hadn't been thirteen days or weeks or even months since he'd seen this woman. Years. Thirteen years. More than a decade. They were different people than they'd been back then. It didn't make one whit of difference how familiar her mouth felt.

"I shouldn't have done that," he said.

"It's fine," she said, dismissing it with a wave of her hand. "Adrenaline."

Well, that certainly sounded better than *lust*. He stared at her.

"It was just a kiss, Brody. Let's forget it. We need to find that water," she said.

It hadn't been just a kiss. It had been a startling hot rush and his body was still humming.

But Elle was acting as if it had been nothing, meant nothing.

He turned and started walking. And by the time they found the stream ten minutes later, his pulse had slowed down and was once again beating pretty normally. The water was running off a ledge of rock that extended from the ravine wall. Brody looked up and tried to trace the flow. "Hard to tell where the source is."

"Which means it may or may not be fresh water," Elle said.

"Which means that finding it is good but we need to boil it before we drink it. I have a couple empty bottles in my bag," he said. "We'll gather it now and boil it tonight when we make camp."

She nodded and held out her hand for a container. "Maybe we should finish off our bottles of water so that they're empty, too. We can collect more then."

He shook his head. "We've got a long walk ahead of us. Let's combine our good water in one bottle and share that. That will give us one more empty."

It took them just a few minutes to hold their bottles under the running stream. Then they crossed the narrow bottom of the ravine and started the hard climb up the steep hill. They were about a third of the way up when it started to rain.

There was no gentle ramp-up to the storm. No little drizzle that turned into a light shower. It was immediate and it was a full-blown drenching. It was as if the damn sky had opened up.

Elle could not even see Brody through the driving rain. She didn't know what to do and had a momentary feeling of panic. She was just getting it under control when she felt a hand on her shoulder.

"Hang on," he said.

He pulled her under a big tree with full foliage. It didn't protect them totally, but it cut the impact of the driving rain. "Wow, that came up fast," Brody said, wiping his streaming face with the back of his forearm.

"It's always like that here. One minute, nothing. The next, a monsoon. We're lucky," she added. "June is the end of our rainy season. If this was March, this ground might be flooded. The Amazon River floods every year."

"I'd rather walk it than swim it."

"Definitely. There are piranhas and anacondas and all kinds of nasty things in the river."

"Not to mention the crocodiles," he added.

The conversation had her glancing down, looking for more snakes. It was hard to see, but nothing popped out at her right away. "I imagine it's going to take me a while to forget the sight of a bushmaster wrapping itself around my feet."

"You handled it like a champ," he said.

"I was this close to wetting my pants," she said. Which reminded him that neither one of them had gone to the bathroom all day. "Do I need to turn my back?"

"No. I think I'm sweating out all my excess water."

He was, too. Which was not good. "How long will this last?"

"Probably not that long. Maybe a half hour. It feels good, but our clothes are going to be damp now, which isn't going to be very comfortable."

He turned to look at her and his gaze settled on her. Her shirt was wet and clinging to her. He could see her full breasts through the thin cotton shirt. Could see the outline of her nipples. She was not wearing a bra.

Hell. One little kiss had made him smolder for hours. This was likely to cause a full-blown implosion.

If somebody took his vitals right now, his temperature would be off the charts. His blood pressure would be screaming stroke.

"I think comfort was ten miles back," he said, his voice husky.

He'd meant it as a casual comment but realized immediately, when she crossed her arms over her chest, that she'd picked up on the double entendre.

"Brody?" she asked.

"What?" he responded innocently. He stuck

out his tongue and tried to catch a few rain drops, hoping to let the awkward moment pass.

It worked. "You look ridiculous," she said. She cupped her hands and held them out from her body. It was raining hard, but still she captured a ridiculously small amount, barely enough to lick off her palms.

"Oh, yeah. Your method is *much* better."

She ignored him. "How do you think they're doing back at the plane?" she asked.

"I think they have shelter and access to water and food. They'll be okay."

"I hope so."

He could hear the uncertainty. "We're going to be okay, too, Elle," he said, suddenly desperately wanting to assure her. "We kept up a good pace today. If we can do the same tomorrow and if your calculations were correct, we should be having a drink with your friend by tomorrow night."

"It's a lot of ifs. And you forgot some. If one of us doesn't twist an ankle. If we don't get sick from bad water. If some native doesn't get mad that we're walking across his family's sacred graveyard, we should be okay."

"Family's sacred graveyard," he repeated, one corner of his mouth lifted.

"You know what I mean," she said, waving her hand.

"I do. I'm just giving you a hard time. Yeah, there's lots of obstacles. But we're tougher."

She let out a loud sigh and was quiet for several minutes. Finally, she pushed her hair back from her face and gave him a smile. "Okay. I think I'm over my pity party. I just needed to get that out of the way."

He stared at her. "You have been incredibly brave, Elle, from the beginning. You're entitled to have a few nagging doubts. It doesn't make you weak."

She looked off into the distance. "If anyone would have told me that I was going to be in a plane crash and have to walk my way out of the Amazon, I'd have laughed at them."

"What if they'd told you that you were going to have to do it with me?"

It took her a full minute to shift her gaze. When she did, her eyes were bright. "I'd have said that it would never happen because whatever direction I walked, Brody Donovan would go the opposite way. Anything to keep some space between the two of us."

"That's not true," he said. Maybe at one time he'd have thought that but not now. Not after seeing Elle in action, not after realizing that she was more than equal to the task. Not after realizing that he…that he still…thought a lot of her.

Chicken.

Maybe. But he wasn't ready to go further than that. Thirteen years ago he'd been dealt a blow, one that might not have been fatal to his other organs but had certainly damaged his heart.

"Brody, you have every reason in the world to hate me."

She'd always had this uncanny ability to read his thoughts. She was on the right track but a little off course. "I never hated you, Elle," he said, his voice cracking on her name. There had been so many emotions following her leaving, but hate hadn't been one of them. He'd loved her too much. "The way you did it was wrong," he said.

"You're right," she said. "I took the coward's way out."

That surprised him. He expected her to have a thousand reasons why that had been the only way she could have done it. "I tried to find you," he admitted. "I talked to your mother, to your stepfather."

Her head whipped his direction. "What did they tell you?"

"Not much. Your mother said that she hadn't spoken to you for months. She didn't recognize my name. I thought that was odd given that we were supposed to be married in just weeks and that we were supposed to be visiting her in days."

Elle blinked rapidly but didn't say anything. That made Brody crazy. He wanted to demand to know the truth. Why hadn't she told her mother about him? Why hadn't she been honest about her relationship with her mother?

When it was apparent that she wasn't going to offer up any explanation, he went on. "Your stepfather said he hadn't heard from you and didn't expect to."

"Hoped," she said.

"What?"

"Hoped he didn't hear from me. Never mind. It would have been difficult to find me. I moved around a lot," she said. "Especially in those first years."

He couldn't imagine not keeping in contact with his parents. Even when he was in Afghanistan and Iraq, he'd stayed in touch through email and regular telephone calls.

She'd been too busy *moving around*. But she'd stayed long enough in one place to get pregnant, to have another man's child. "What happened to your daughter's father?" he asked.

She looked startled, as if that hadn't been the

question she'd been expecting. "He's...dead," she said.

He was a bad person because even that didn't make him hate the man any less. Elle had loved him enough to have his child. "I'm sorry," he managed.

She didn't say anything until finally she lifted her pretty chin. "So is her mother."

What? And Brody's thoughts might have been a little sluggish from general dehydration, but it still clicked into place. "She's adopted? Your daughter is adopted?"

"Yes," she whispered. "Mia is a student at the school where I teach. Her parents were killed in a bus accident several years ago and she'd been living in an orphanage since that time. I adopted her about a year ago."

"Mia," he repeated. "Did you know her parents?"

She shook her head. "No. Mia has a few pictures of them. They seemed like a happy family. She has lost a lot. But she's very, very brave."

It seemed sort of an odd way to describe a child. "She's not afraid of snakes?" he asked.

She smiled. "I'm not sure about that. Look, the rain has stopped. We need to get going."

Secrets. Half-truths. Elle was a master at them.

She shut people out.

Because a heart could only take so much, especially a damaged one, he turned and started walking.

Chapter Nine

By four in the afternoon, Elle felt as if she didn't have the strength or the energy to put one foot in front of the other. But she kept moving, knowing that Brody had to be as weary. When it was impossible to go around foliage, he'd had the extra burden of using Mrs. Hardy's knife to saw through dense palms and other plant life. It was painstakingly slow and she grew agitated, knowing that nightfall was edging closer every minute.

The heat was sweltering and her clothes were sticking to her. She could smell herself and it wasn't pretty. It was some disgusting combination of sweat and the bug repellant that she'd reapplied after the rain stopped. Her hair felt heavy and even though she tried to push it away from her face, pieces clung to her neck.

Her shoulders and arms ached because, after the snake incident, she taken to swinging her sturdy walking stick in front of her every time there was a patch of long grass or undergrowth to walk through. Unfortunately, that had meant a lot of swinging.

She had a raging headache. Probably because she was dehydrated and probably because she was still whirling from Brody's statement that he'd talked to both her mother and stepfather.

She'd called her mother a month after she was in Peru. Hadn't told her where she was living. Her mother hadn't mentioned that she'd spoken to Brody. Hadn't mentioned that a fiancé she didn't know about had called.

She would have been surprised if her mother had been chatty with Brody. Catherine Rivers wasn't going to talk about something that had happened all those years ago. Talking about it would make it real, and that was something that she was never going to admit.

Same for Earl Rivers, the man who had been her stepfather for three years.

She hadn't really thought it through that Brody might attempt to contact her family. The idea that he'd spoken to her mother was hard to get her head around, and the idea that he'd had to lower himself to have a conversation with Earl Rivers was so distasteful that she had to swallow hard to keep her empty stomach from jumping.

"We'll need to make camp soon," Brody said. "The sun will set shortly after five."

She was grateful for the interruption. Thinking about Rivers wasn't going to help her headache go away.

"If I stop walking, there is a distinct possibility that I may never start again," Elle said.

She felt compelled to say something because it was the first thing Brody had said to her since they resumed walking after the rain. She'd been shaken when he mentioned talking to her mother and stepfather. Then when he abruptly switched the topic to Mia, she'd been so startled that she blurted out information. Not that it was difficult to talk about the little girl who had become so important to her over the past year. Mia was a delight. Beautiful. Funny. Polite. Brave, as she'd said.

Thank goodness for the last trait. If not for Mia's bravery, Elle might never have realized the truth about T. K. Jamas. And once Elle had discovered the truth, nothing would have stopped her from testifying against Jamas, not even when the man had threatened to kill both her and Mia.

With Father Taquero's help, she'd safely hidden Mia away. Nobody was going to find her until Elle could get her out of the country.

And while intellectually she knew that Brody was absolutely no threat to Mia, when he'd started asking questions, Elle shut down.

Mia's safety was too important. She couldn't let something slip to Brody that might compromise her little girl's safety. Elle knew all too well what it was like to be young and vulnerable and to be in the care of adults that were careless about a child's safety. She knew all too well that sometimes a child's pleas for protection could go ignored.

But she needed to not dwell on that right now. Every bit of her energy had to be focused on putting one foot in front of the other before her legs cramped up from overuse and lack of water.

A half hour later, she saw a possibility. "Brody, what about this?" she said, pointing to a small rise. There were a couple palm trees close together that might work for tying up the parachute-turned-hammock. Also a couple small plants, but otherwise the little hill was clear of foliage.

Brody studied the space and nodded. "Looks good to me."

Good. Well, not exactly. Off and on throughout the day, she'd thought about spending the night in the jungle, and the concept hadn't improved with time or distance. The two nights that she'd slept in the plane were bad enough. She'd heard the howl of wild animals, and even the knowledge that the plane would be an effective deterrent had not made her feel much better.

Tonight, she and Brody would be vulnerable, and that scared the heck out of her. But she wasn't going to admit that. She knew enough to avoid being near a water source. That would attract all kinds of animals. And they needed to be somewhere that offered some protection if it decided to rain again.

"Let's gather wood on our way," Brody said.

Definitely. She intended to keep the fire burning all night. That would also be a useful deterrent to unwanted visitors. She reached down to pick up a log and realized when her hand was just inches away that there was a hairy spider, three times the size of her thumbnail, staring at her.

She jumped back.

And she must have squealed because Brody whirled.

"It's okay," she said, holding up a shaking hand. "Spider. Big enough that it probably eats small children for breakfast."

"One of those," he said, nodding solemnly. He started walking again.

She held her breath as she walked by the log, as if that would somehow protect her. After that, she viewed each piece of wood critically before poking it with her stick. Then she pounded one end on the ground, to dislodge any stubborn bugs or spiders, before picking it up.

It took a while, but by the time they reached the top of the hill, she had an armload of wood that looked as if it would burn. Night was fast approaching and Brody quickly made his circle and stacked the wood for a fire. It caught with the first match. He carefully put the book of matches back in the small plastic bag and back in his shirt pocket.

She helped him unfold the parachute and string it between two trees. They tied it tight using the suspension lines. There was the section missing that Elle had cut out that first night, but that was at the very end. Brody would simply have to be careful or his feet would fall through.

"Get in," Brody said, surprising her. "Test it."

She supposed she could. She sat her rear down and swung her legs up, then lay back, one arm folded underneath her head. She raised her other hand and motioned with her finger. "Waiter, can you bring me another rum smoothie?"

Brody laughed, and it sounded so much like the old Brody laugh that she couldn't help laughing along with him. It was contagious and pretty soon, the two of them were whooping it up like a bunch of hyenas.

It probably lasted less than a minute, but the absolute joy that flooded her system was a welcome relief from the strain of the past two days. "That felt good," she admitted.

"It did." He stared down at her, his gaze intense.

Was he remembering all the times they had laughed together? Like when they read the *New Yorker* magazine together and came across a joke that cracked them up. Or when they used to lie in bed for hours on his rare free day with a pile of DVDs of the latest comedies? Watching. Laughing. Making love in between.

She swung her feet over the side of the hammock, sat up, then stood quickly. "We should probably boil water. Before it's totally dark."

They used Mrs. Hardy's small coffeepot. They'd collected three bottles' worth from the stream, and that meant that they had to boil six batches. It was a tedious process because they had to wait for each batch to cool before they could pour it back into plastic bottles. There was very little to do besides stare at the fire.

"Tell me about your school," Brody said after some time.

"We have about a hundred students, both boys and girls, all between the ages of ten and thirteen. Some from families that might be middle-class. Most from poor families and they receive assistance from the church. I teach English and they're all eager to learn. These are children who realize that education is their way out of poverty, to have a better life."

"Sounds like rewarding work. You're making a difference in those kids' lives."

She felt warm and she didn't think it was due to the fire. "I hope so."

When the last batch was cooling, Brody pulled a tea bag out of his duffel bag and held it up for Elle to see. "Join me for a cup of tea?" he said, as if they'd just happened to meet each other at the corner bistro.

"Love to," she said.

He dropped the tea bag into the glass pot and after a minute or so, poured the still-warm liquid into one of their plastic water bottles. They took turns sipping tea out of the bottle while they split their one breakfast bar and slowly chewed it and a handful of nuts. There was something so civilized about drinking tea that it was almost possible to forget that they were in the middle of nowhere, surrounded by wild, poisonous things.

Although the mosquitoes were doing their best to remind them that it was their jungle first. "We're going to get eaten alive," Elle said, swatting at one on her sleeve. She pulled the mosquito repellent out of her backpack. "Better put a little more of this on for the night."

They both put it on the faces and necks.

"We should get some sleep," he said.

She opened her backpack and pulled out the newspaper and the blanket. She found a spot between the fire and Brody's hammock and put the papers on the ground.

"What are you doing?" he asked.

"I'm going to sit on the papers and wrap myself up in the blanket. Then I'm going to sleep."

He shook his head. "The hammock is for you."

She pulled back in surprise. "No. You carried it all day. You should get the benefit of sleeping in it."

"Don't be ridiculous," he said. "I'm not going to take the hammock while you're on the ground."

"Why not?" she challenged, knowing it was a stupid thing to fight about, but she couldn't help herself.

The fire gave off enough light that she could see him roll his eyes. "Take the hammock, Elle."

She couldn't let it go. "But what about you?"

He waved a hand. "Don't worry about me.

I was a Boy Scout. I know how to sleep on the ground."

She shook her head. "It's not a matter of being tough enough. There are poisonous creepy crawlers in the jungle. If there's a way for you to sleep off the ground, you need to do it."

"Creepy crawlers," he repeated.

"Too numerous to mention," she said. "The hammock was a good idea. It's yours."

"Nope."

"Rock, paper, scissors?" she asked sarcastically.

"Nope," he repeated.

They were getting nowhere. "Oh, for goodness' sake. Then we'll share it."

He shook his head. "Hammocks aren't exactly meant for two people, Elle," he said.

"Well, we're going to have to figure out a way to make it work. You get in first."

He blew out a long breath, sat down in it and stretched out. "Okay. It should hold both of us. Get in."

His tone was exasperated, not at all tender, yet it made it remember how he used to get in bed before she did on really cold nights and warm up the sheets because she absolutely hated to climb into a cold bed. *Time to get in, darling.* That's what he would say.

She sat on the edge of the hammock and tried to lie down, her back to his back. However, the weight distribution was all wrong and the hammock would have turned over on itself and likely ripped off the trees if he hadn't moved pretty quickly and somehow vaulted out of the hammock into a standing position.

"That's not going to work," he said, looking down at her.

She realized that if any animals were watching them, they were giving them quite a show. *Look, see, the human circus has come to town.*

Feet to head wouldn't work because of the missing section of parachute. The only position that would really work was him spooning her.

He must have come to the same realization. Or maybe he'd known it all along. "It's not too late," he said.

"Don't be ridiculous," she said, throwing his earlier words back at him. She got out of the hammock and motioned for him to get back in.

He did.

Then like an Amazonian princess, with her chin held high, she got into her bed, her back to his front.

The only logical place for his right arm was under her head, and for his left, resting lightly on her hip.

She pretended that it didn't even bother her

that she could feel him everywhere. His thighs against her thighs. His chest against her back. His breath against her neck.

His groin against her rear.

The Amazonian princess wanted to squirm. But she held herself rigidly still. Like royalty.

"Everything okay?" he asked, a hint of challenge in his voice.

"It's fine. Just pull the blanket up and let's get some sleep. Please."

He did as instructed. The blanket came up to their necks, but he evidently didn't want to leave their heads exposed. He hooked an arm around his bag and pulled it close. Then he opened it, pulled out his extra shirt, and carefully zipped his bag back up. He draped the shirt over their heads and part of their faces, leaving their mouths and noses free but relatively nothing else uncovered.

She'd thought she couldn't possibly sleep. But within minutes, she felt the overpowering need for rest consume her body. And she let go.

And didn't wake up until she heard the bone-chilling cry of an animal, or several animals, off in the distance. Angry, threatening sounds. She stiffened.

"It's okay," he murmured, his voice close to her ear, his voice sleepy. "Sound carries at night. They aren't that close."

She realized that at some point in the night, instead of rigidly trying to keep a thin line of demarcation between the two of them, she'd slipped into his embrace. She waited for him to realize it, to stiffen, to pull away.

Instead, he tucked her in tighter.

And in the middle of a dark Amazon rain forest, a tear leaked out of her eye because of all she had given up.

THE NEXT TIME she woke up, she was all alone in the hammock. It was light out and Brody was standing by the fire, his back to her. The angle was right that she could see he had his arms folded over his chest and was deep in thought.

She didn't want to intrude. She'd given up the right to his thoughts many years before.

He turned, as if he had somehow sensed she was awake. He stared at her. "Good morning," he said, his voice rusty.

"Good morning."

"There's tea," he said.

"Thank you." She reached over the side of the hammock, grabbed the end of her walking stick that she'd placed there the night before, and tapped and swished it around on the ground, giving the vermin in the area fair warning that she was about to get up.

Brody watched her and she could see a slight smile at the corner of his mouth.

Great. She was amusing.

When she got close enough, he handed her the tea bottle and she took a drink. The liquid was still warm and she thought it might have been the best cup of tea that she'd ever had.

The breakfast bar and nuts were gone, but with any luck, they'd find bananas and berries that would sustain them for the journey. By tonight, if her calculations were correct, they'd be sitting around Leo's table.

As if he could read her thoughts, Brody turned to her. "Tell me about your friend that we're looking for."

"His name is Leo Arroul. I've known him for more than ten years. We regularly keep in touch online and see each other every couple of years. He's very smart, maybe not as smart as you, but smart."

"I'm not that smart," he said.

"Right. Anyway, he had a big corporate job at one time but now he works on developing clean water systems."

"Is he married?"

It was an odd question. It took her a minute to realize that Brody was fishing, that what he really wanted to know was whether there was something more than friendship between her and Leo. "Not anymore. Divorced some time ago. We've never had that kind of relationship." She dug the toe of her loafer into the dew-covered dirt. "I haven't had that kind of relationship with anybody," she said. "I didn't leave you for someone else," she added, suddenly believing it was very important for him to know that.

There was a long moment of silence before he turned to her. His eyes were bright. "Why did you leave, Elle? What was so wrong that you had to run away, three weeks before our wedding?" His voice sounded strangled.

She could not say a word.

"You know, my mother had to return all the gifts that people had already sent. Everyone said how badly they felt for me. *Poor Brody. Left at the altar.* That's what they said. People pitied me, Elle. I hated that."

"I'm sorry," she whispered. "I...I didn't think," she admitted. She'd acted. Not necessarily on impulse. No, it had been too important for that. But once she'd decided, she'd acted fast, scared that she wasn't strong enough.

Strong enough to leave him.

"That's it. That's your whole explanation. *I didn't think.*"

She shook her head. "Does it really matter, Brody? What's done is done. I'm sorry I hurt

you. I'm sorry I didn't handle it better. Happy?"
She knew she sounded angry and antagonistic
when in truth she was simply heartsick.

"Happy?" he repeated incredulously. He
didn't say anything for a long minute. Finally,
he spoke. "Yep. Happy as a duck in water. Now
let's go."

Chapter Ten

Brody set an aggressive pace and, to her credit, Elle kept up. However, two hours into their morning, their pace slowed considerably. The tree and plant growth was substantially heavier, making it impossible to easily skirt around obstacles. There was no choice but to go through it, and Mrs. Hardy's knife wasn't really up to the task.

Sweat ran down his back from the exertion of sawing through plants. His shoulders hurt and he had a four-inch rip in his shirt where the sharp end of a plant had collided with his arm. Fortunately, he'd jerked back in time to avoid a deep cut in his skin.

"If the rest of the way is like this, we aren't going to make your friend's house by nightfall."

She nodded, her hands on her hips. Her breath was labored from the difficulty of getting through the thick growth.

"We just have to keep going," she said. "Every step is one step closer."

He appreciated her optimism, but it was likely they might have to spend another night in the jungle.

Another night in the hammock with Elle.

Great. Probably add another couple years to how long it would take to get over her this time.

He put his head down and concentrated on putting one foot in front of the other. But five minutes later, he stopped. And listened.

Over the years, his senses had become finely attuned to the sounds of helicopters bringing wounded to the base medical camp. He could be in a dead sleep and somehow, he would wake up.

"What?" Elle asked, scanning the bushes and trees, probably thinking he'd seen something dangerous.

He almost didn't want to tell her, didn't want to get her hopes up. "Helicopter. Do you hear it?"

She stood very still and looked up. A minute later, she grinned. "I do. Oh, God. I do."

Brody stopped to unzip his bag. "I'm going to grab the parachute. It's the brightest thing we have. Maybe they will be able to see it from the air. There's no place to land, but at least they'll see us and know we're here."

When she didn't answer, he looked up and realized that she'd run ahead, probably trying to get to a spot where they could see her.

Brody's heart was thumping in his chest. He'd been confident that he and Elle had the stamina and the will to make it out of the jungle. But stamina and will could get sidelined fast by a bite from a poisonous spider or a broken ankle or any number of things that could happen on a stroll through the jungle. The helicopter coming was a great relief.

It would mean saying goodbye to Elle again.

He tried to push away the despair that settled over him. She'd probably be terribly relieved. She hadn't spoken to him in over two hours after he'd verbally beaten her over the head this morning.

The helicopter was closer. Off to the left, above the tree line. Then he saw it. Dipping and swaying, avoiding the trees, obviously looking for something on the ground.

Looking for them. He started to run, hoping to catch up with Elle.

And, then, through a thin slit in the thick canopy of trees, he saw something incredible happen.

The helicopter stopped weaving and hovered and its side door opened. A man appeared.

Then Brody saw the big gun.

And it took him just a second to realize that the man was shooting.

At Elle.

SHE RAN INTO Brody hard enough that it knocked the wind out of her. Then he was yanking on her arm, dragging her behind one of the bigger trees in the deep foliage.

"What the hell?" he said.

If he expected an answer, he was out of luck. That man in the helicopter had been *shooting* at her. No one had ever shot at her before.

They could hear the helicopter hovering above, close enough that it was stirring the air and leaves were whirling. But what Brody had been bemoaning just minutes earlier was now saving their bacon. They were safely hidden and there was no place to land.

T. K. Jamas. It had to be him. He had the resources to organize a private rescue effort and he had much to lose if she testified against him.

It was quite frankly almost impossible to get her head around the idea that the man had seen her, lifted his gun and started shooting. By some miracle, the first shot had landed at her feet. Whether it had been the fault of the pilot or the shooter, she was grateful. It had given her a chance to run and the next three shots had missed as well.

"I'm so sorry," she said. "This is all because of me."

He stared at her, emotion flashing in his eyes. "Talk fast, Elle," he said. "What the hell do you mean?"

"It's a very long story. I'm on my way back to the States to testify against a man who at one time I trusted very much. I discovered that he was leading a human-trafficking ring and that most of his victims were eleven-and twelve-year-old girls. I think he may be determined that I don't ever get a chance to tell my story."

"His name," Brody said, his tone insistent.

"T. K. Jamas. He's Peruvian but has lived in Brazil for many years."

Brody looked as if he had a hundred other questions but, to his credit, he didn't ask them. When they heard the sound of the helicopter fading, he grabbed her hand. "Let's go," he said. "We need to get away from here. If you're right, that helicopter is going to look for the closest space where they can land safely and then pursue us on foot."

She hadn't thought she could get any more terrified.

"I dropped my bag and the parachute when I saw that man shooting at you. Stay here while I get it," he said.

She managed a nod.

While Brody was gone, the monkeys in the trees chattered at her, mad that she was in their space, mad that she'd brought the noisy beast with the rotating blades to their home.

Brody was the one who had a right to be furious. When he came back, she put her hand on his arm. "We need to separate. You keep going east. I'm going to head north."

"But you said that your friend would help you."

"I'm not going to lead Jamas to Leo's door," she said, shaking her head. "It's bad enough that I've dragged you into my troubles. You need to get away. I don't think there's any way they could have seen you. You need to keep going, find Leo, and he'll help you."

"Stop talking," Brody said.

"What?"

"I said, stop talking. If you're only going to talk nonsense, then I don't want to hear anything."

Nonsense. She was trying to save his life. "Listen to me," she said. "I think it's possible that Jamas was responsible for the crash."

"What?"

"Captain Ramano seemed mad at me and made odd comments that made me think that he thought I was responsible for the crash. He also knew about the school where I teach.

Maybe Jamas paid Captain Ramano to crash the plane?"

Brody shook his head. "That doesn't make sense. It's a bad business proposition. Ramano was as likely to die as anyone else in a plane crash."

Elle tried to think. "All I know is that Captain Ramano acted oddly toward me."

"Not good enough," Brody said. He grabbed her hand. "Let's go."

She took about ten steps before stopping. "What if Jamas was somehow responsible for the crash and he wanted to verify that everyone had died? What if he found the plane? He's a horrible man. He may have killed everyone."

Brody put his hands in the air. "I hope to hell you're wrong, but right now we can't think about that. We need to focus our energies on safely getting out of this jungle without anybody else shooting at us. We're close to Mantau and to your friend Leo. We have to keep going. There's no other choice."

"But—"

"We're not separating," he said. "End of discussion. Is there any reason to think that Jamas knows that you would seek help from Leo?"

She thought. Had she ever mentioned Leo to Jamas? She didn't think so. "No. But he knows the jungle well. He knows that Mantau is the closest village. He might suspect that I'm headed that way. He might also think, however, that I'm headed toward a river. That's always the fastest way to travel in the jungle."

"Okay, then we stay on course. We're going to need to pick up the pace even more and if we hear the helicopter, make sure we stay out of sight."

She put her hand on his arm. "I'm sorry. I feel as if I'm destined to keep telling you that and I'm sure you aren't all that impressed with my apologies, but I am truly sorry."

He shook his head. "Elle, let's just focus on the here and now. I think that's about the best I can do. It sounds as if you're trying to do a very good thing. You're trying to make a monster pay for his crimes. You don't have to apologize."

For that, she added silently. But he was right. Now wasn't the time. They were literally running for their lives.

Two hours later, hot, exhausted and filthy, Elle almost welcomed the afternoon rain that hit with a vengeance. But Brody didn't stop. Twice, they'd heard the helicopter and it had hovered over the thick canopy of trees, but still Brody had pushed ahead. He'd stopped marking the trail with the red strips of cloth. It would make it more difficult to find their way back to the plane but more difficult for Jamas to track them, as well.

She stepped over a rotting log and her foot slipped on the long wet grass. She went down.

Strong hands picked her up. "Are you hurt?" Brody asked, his voice close to her ear. Water ran down his face.

"My knee," she said. "Went down hard on it. It'll be fine."

He knelt in front her, pulled her pants out of her dirty socks, and lifted up the wet material. With practiced hands, he felt around her leg, her knee. His skin was warm against her cold, wet legs.

"It looks okay," he said. "Can you walk?" He stood up.

"Were you going to carry me?" she asked, trying to put a little levity into a very grim situation.

"I'll do what I have to do," he said.

It was the same thing he'd said when faced with the possibility of operating on Captain Ramano when there was concern about internal injuries.

Brody Donovan was that kind of guy. He'd do what he needed to do to get the job done.

"I can walk," she said. "We have to be very close, maybe less than an hour from Mantau. As I recall, there are several trails that lead from the village into the jungle. The jungle provides many of the raw materials that the villagers use to survive and to eke out small livings. Once we hit one of those trails, we're going to start to see people. We'll need to be careful."

"Why?"

"Jamas has a lot of money. I suspect that he's already sent someone this direction, waving a handful of money, probably more than these people make in six months, asking for information about me. There's no way that they wouldn't turn us in for that kind of money."

She could see the frustration on his face. Understood it.

"So we *are* going to need to split up," she said. "I'll stay back in the jungle while you go into town. Find Leo and come back for me."

"No. I'm not leaving you," he said.

"You have to. It's the safest way. For you. For both of us."

He looked as if he wanted to argue. Then he evidently changed his mind and before she realized what was happening, he was kissing her, his mouth hard, insistent.

They were filthy, in the middle of a steaming-hot jungle, with bad men chasing them, and she forgot it all. She was lost in the wonder of his kiss. The total abandon of caution.

She opened her mouth and welcomed his

tongue. She pressed her body against his. Every curve fit, every touch burned.

"Oh, Brody," she said when he finally lifted his head.

"Elle," he whispered. "you have been amazing these last two days. So strong. So wise. I can't imagine anyone who might have handled it better."

She felt warm. There had been a time when praise like that from Brody would have meant everything to her. But now it was too late. Too much time had passed. They were different people.

She felt him lift her shirt and put the palm of his hand on her back. With his index finger, he traced her spine.

It didn't feel different. It felt dazzlingly familiar.

He kissed her for a very long time. Finally, he lifted his head. "You keep apologizing but I'm the one who should be sorry," he said. "I've been an ass toward you. I had thirteen years to get over being mad. I don't know what got into me. I saw you and suddenly I was twenty-five again and all those old feelings came rushing back at me. It wasn't fair to you. You had a right to end it."

"I may have had a right, but I did it badly."

"You were young."

He was right. Just twenty-one. "It was a long time ago," she said.

Could he forgive her? Could she forgive herself?

He held her. Tight. And she rested her head against his shoulder. "You should go," she said finally. "You need to get into the village and back again before it gets dark."

"I don't want to leave you," he said. "Not with those men looking for you."

"I'll be safe," she said. "I'll stay hidden."

He kissed her again. More tenderly this time, more sensuously. He slid his hand from her back to her stomach, then up, until the pad of his thumb brushed across her nipple.

The sensation shot to her core and she wanted him with an intensity that she had not felt in many, many years. Thirteen years.

She arched her back. He raised her shirt, exposing her breast to the warm air, holding the weight of it in his hand.

"So pretty," he murmured. His kisses traveled down her neck.

And when he took her breast in his mouth, her legs would have crumpled had he not been supporting her. "I smell," she protested weakly.

"Wonderful," he said.

She could feel him, his erection straining

at his pants, pushing at her. She wanted him desperately.

But there was no time. "Brody," she said, stepping away. She pulled down her shirt. "You have to go."

He shook his head, as if to clear it. "I know, damn it. I know," he added, his tone rueful. He looked in her eyes. "I'll find your friend and we'll be back. And you damn well better be here."

BRODY CHANGED INTO his last clean shirt before he walked into Mantau. Elle was right in that the men in the helicopter probably hadn't seen him. But if they had come upon the plane wreckage and talked to the other survivors, then they knew that Elle was not alone.

He carried his water bottle in one hand and his walking stick in the other. He had Mrs. Hardy's knife in his pocket.

He and Elle had discussed whether he should take the knife or leave it with her. In the end, she'd won, insisting that she intended to stay hidden, that she wouldn't need the knife, while he still had an hour's worth of jungle to navigate and the knife might be absolutely necessary.

He encountered his first person less than thirty minutes from where he'd left Elle in the jungle. He was a thin, dark-skinned man, wearing a big straw hat and carrying a small shovel.

The man paid no attention to him and Brody let out a sigh of relief. Another fifteen minutes later, there were two women, both with tan blouses, long dark skirts and sandals. They carried baskets. They rested their gaze on him and he nodded politely in their direction but didn't break stride.

It was frightening and exhilarating at the same time to finally see other humans. It had been almost seventy hours since the plane crashed and more than once in that time, when he'd been surrounded by trees and plants, with no trail in sight, he'd doubted that this would be the eventual outcome.

He wanted to run up to them and demand to know whether they knew Leo Arroul, but he waited. Elle had been right about almost everything so far. If she believed that people might be looking for American strangers, then he didn't intend to raise their curiosity more than absolute necessary.

The village of Mantau was less than fifteen minutes down the dirt road that would only have been wide enough for one American car. But there were no cars. There were people pulling three-wheeled carts, but that was the extent of the moving vehicles.

There were probably twenty-five small square bamboo huts, all on risers so that their front doors were at least six steps up. All had thatch roofs. Most had a porch of some kind and he was close enough that on one, he could see an old woman using a brick fireplace to cook a fish with its head still on.

He kept walking. On a street in roughly the middle of town, there were two stands akin to the hot-dog vendor he loved in New York, without the hot dogs or wheels on their stands. On the right was a young woman who had raw fish and baked bread on her counter. Next to her was a much older man selling fresh fruit, vegetables and something that resembled hard brown sugar.

Jungle commerce.

He reached into his pocket and fingered a real. He had exchanged dollars for the Brazilian currency at the bank before boarding the plane in Miami. Before leaving the plane with Elle, he'd made sure he had the money with him. Everywhere in the world, money talked.

And right now he wanted the young woman to feel chatty.

He admired her bread and selected a long, flat loaf that would be easy to carry. She wrapped it in tan paper that she secured with a piece of string.

"Obrigado," he said. Thank you was about the extent of his Portuguese. She smiled and put the money in her skirt pocket.

"Do you speak English?" he asked.

She shrugged. "Some," she said with a heavy accent.

He took a deep breath. "I am looking for an old friend. His name is Leo Arroul. Do you know him?"

Chapter Eleven

She smiled wider this time and he noticed that one of her eyeteeth was missing. She raised her arm and pointed to a building at the end of the street, on the left side. "Leo," she said. "Good man."

He could feel his heart start to race in his chest. But he contained his energy, much like before he did a very complex surgery. *"Obrigado,"* he repeated.

He turned and caught the stare of the man selling the fruit. A frisson of unease settled between his shoulder blades, but he ignored it. He walked at the same pace that he had used when entering the village. It took him ninety-three steps to reach Leo's front door.

He knocked and waited. The door opened and there was an older man, maybe close to sixty, wearing wrinkled cotton pants and a matching shirt. He was completely bald. He had friendly brown eyes.

"Are you Leo Arroul?" Brody asked.

The man nodded.

Brody looked over the man's shoulder. There was no one else inside the small one-room house. "My name is Brody Donovan. I am a friend of Elle Vollman. She needs your help."

Leo pulled him inside and offered him something to drink. Brody drank the water and then filled up his water bottle, intending to take it back for Elle. He quickly told Leo about the plane crash, the walk through the jungle, the helicopter and the men shooting at Elle.

When he said the name T. K. Jamas, Leo's eyebrows shot up.

"Do you know him?" Brody asked.

"I have met him," Leo said. "He can be quite charming. I wish I'd known that Elle was involved with him. I'd have warned her."

Brody started to argue that Elle wasn't *involved* with Jamas but then realized it wasn't important. What was important was getting back to Elle and getting her safely to the United States.

"Elle believes that he's involved in human trafficking."

Leo did not look surprised. His next statement, however, took Brody off guard. "Jamas has a home somewhere near here. I'm not exactly sure where. I've never been interested enough to find out. I believe it belonged to his father and Jamas is only there occasionally."

"I don't think Elle had any idea that he had any connections to this area. She would never have come this direction."

"Well, then, I'm glad she didn't know. I can help you. But how did you find me?" Leo asked.

"I asked the young woman who was selling bread, just down the street."

"Did anyone hear you?" Leo asked.

"I think the man behind the other stand might have."

Leo nodded and stood up. "Then we must hurry. We might not have much time."

"What?" Brody demanded.

"His name is Paulo and let's just say he's easily influenced by others. And most easily influenced by money. If it's known that Jamas will pay for information about Elle, then Paulo would be in line for the money."

"I never said her name."

"You wouldn't have to. You are American. Elle is American. I am perceived to be American, even though I am really Canadian. That would be enough."

"Let's go. It could take an hour to get back."

Leo grabbed a large black backpack off a hook near the door. He filled it with mangoes and bananas from the bowl on his table. Then he opened a container on the table and pulled out something wrapped in white paper. Finally, he opened the door of a freestanding cupboard and retrieved several items that Brody couldn't clearly see and added them to the backpack. The last thing he did was sling the strap of a machete over one shoulder.

They did not walk past the fruit stand on their way out of town. Leo turned the opposite direction. Brody took a fast look down the street before they left and he did not see Paulo at his stand.

And while he knew there could be many explanations for the man's absence, Brody could not shake the fear that Paulo was contacting Jamas. Money talked, after all.

Leo led him out of the village and around the small collection of houses. Brody's strides were long, his pace fast.

"Slow down," Leo said, barely moving his mouth. "We're out for a stroll. Two old friends."

Brody forced himself to slow down, to appear relaxed. He glanced at the birds in the trees, at the brilliantly colored flowers that bloomed everywhere.

He watched to see if anyone was following them or taking a particular interest in them but saw nothing that concerned him. It would be okay. He and Elle would be okay.

"Perhaps it's best that we don't tell Elle that I've seen Jamas in Mantau before," Leo said.

Brody shook his head. "We need to tell her. She needs to know everything."

Leo shrugged. "Maybe you're right. Forewarned is forearmed."

When they finally passed a bend in the road that protected them from view of the village, Leo turned to him. "Are you a runner?" the man asked.

Brody nodded.

Leo started off jogging and quickly picked up the pace. "I gained forty pounds after my wife left me," he said. "Then I realized an early death from heart disease wasn't going to hurt her and I started running."

Whatever the reason, Brody was grateful. He would soon be back with Elle.

ELLE HATED THE JUNGLE. She'd come to that conclusion about six minutes after she'd watched Brody walk away. It was noisy and damp and too green.

She was tired and she desperately wanted to sit down, but she was scared to—something would bite her on her butt, it would swell up, Brody would have to administer first aid, and he'd see the cellulite that hadn't been there thirteen years ago.

While it was hard to know exactly how much cellulite might be there, it was not a stretch of the imagination to imagine that there must be some. After all, her legs were not those of a twenty-one-year-old college student who went to the gym every day and cocktailed most nights. Her arms? Well, she saw some jiggle the other day. Her neck. She didn't even want to talk about that.

You're thirty-four, not sixty-four, she told herself. If sixty was the new forty, then thirty-four was the new fourteen. Great. If she slept with Brody, it'd be illegal.

If she slept with Brody. She repeated the words in her head and let them simmer there, in her half-baked brain. Wasn't that presumptuous of her? She was jumping way down the track. Sure, he'd had a physical reaction to her. But maybe that was just because he'd been busy and hadn't had sex for thirteen years?

Who was she kidding? Of course he'd had sex. She had, after all. At least once every two years, that's what she'd told Father Taquero when the two of them were sipping bad wine in the back of the church late one Saturday afternoon.

He'd assured her that was barely worth a Hail Mary.

Even so, after he'd left to get ready for evening mass, she'd added a couple of Our Fathers just to hedge her bets.

The men had been decent guys that she'd met either through her work or through friends. But none of them had been Brody.

And so even the ones who had called several times afterward, she'd politely turned down. And in the past year she hadn't even dated because she'd had Mia, the absolute sweetest little eleven-year-old.

And as Father Taquero was fond of saying, God willing and if the creek don't rise, she and Mia would soon be safe in the United States and they would build a new life together.

But first she needed to get out of the jungle.

Which brought her thoughts full circle to where they'd started when her mind had contemplated cellulite on her rear end. She looked at her watch. Brody had been gone for almost forty minutes. Time enough for him to reach the village and inquire about Leo.

Please, please, let Leo be home. There were times when he was in the depths of the jungle, teaching natives about the importance of clean water and how to test their water using his little strips.

It would be dark in a half hour and that would make it very difficult for Brody to find her. He'd said that he wouldn't mark the trail, but rather he'd find her through several prominent landmarks. But landmarks easily got out of focus when the sun went down.

She saw a sudden burst of white birds, as if they'd been scared up from a tree. She looked. Was that bush moving? Did she hear something?"

There were sounds from her left.

She whirled.

Only to turn back quickly.

Brody and Leo emerged from the jungle. She didn't think she'd ever seen a more welcome sight. And without thinking, she ran toward them and it seemed the most natural thing in the world to get caught up in Brody's strong arms.

"You made it," she murmured, her mouth against his neck.

"Of course," he said, his voice soft. "I wasn't going to leave you out here in the jungle."

His touch felt warm and safe and she didn't want to pull away. But she forced herself to.

"Leo," she said. "I can't begin to tell you how wonderful it is to see you." She stepped close to her friend and gave him a hug.

"It's always wonderful, Elle, but knowing just a little of what you've been through in the last three days, it's better than usual. I am grateful that we found you. Brody was confident, but I was getting concerned that it would soon be too dark."

"We have to tell the authorities about the crash," Elle said.

"Of course," Leo replied. "I've been thinking about that on the way here. Brody told me about your trouble with Jamas. You know he's a very evil man?"

"I do now," Elle replied. "Did Brody tell you about the man in the helicopter?"

"Yes."

"I'm confident that was Jamas's doing. I didn't want to drag you into this, Leo, but I didn't have any choice."

The man waved a hand. "Nonsense. Of course you should have come to me. But we'll need to be very careful. Jamas's family has a home in this area. As I told Brody, I'm not exactly sure where but I've heard it is north of Mantau, near where our small river merges into the Amazon."

Elle shook her head. "You've got to be kidding me. Of all places."

Leo did another hand wave. That was clearly his favorite gesture. "I don't believe he's here very often. But in any event, it would be best if you and Brody could keep a low profile until we can safely move you out of the country."

Brody stepped forward. "How do we do that and lead the authorities to the crash?"

"There is someone I trust in the local government. I'll tell him that I received an anonymous tip about the crash. You indicated that you marked the trail up until a few hours ago. If I give them the approximate location and the trail is marked, they should be able to find the wreckage."

"Will they believe you?"

"I think so. Because of my work with the natives, I often get information that people in more official positions cannot easily obtain. I use my discretion about which information I pass on."

Elle stepped forward and gave her friend another quick hug. "I kept telling Brody that you would help us. Thank you so much."

"You're quite welcome. And while I'd love to invite you back to my home for a meal and some rest, I don't think that's a good idea. Brody may have been overheard asking about me. I don't want to take the chance that Jamas will be watching my house and see the two of you."

A meal and rest, even if the rest was on a wooden floor, sounded heavenly, but she knew that Leo was right. She would handle another night in the jungle. "I understand," she said.

"I have someplace you can go," Leo said. "A house. Outside the village, in a very private area. I…I have a…friend. A special friend. She lives in Costa Rica with her husband and grown children. While that's a substantial distance, her husband is a very powerful businessman, so when she is able to visit, we still must be very discreet."

Elle was happy for her friend. He'd been terribly hurt when his wife left him so many years before. And the offer of shelter for the night sounded heavenly. But she could not afford to make any mistakes. "Are you sure it will be safe?"

"I am. Fortunately, we're already halfway there. It shouldn't take us more than another forty-five minutes to walk there, but it's going to be dark soon and forty-five minutes in the jungle at night is a long time."

"We can do it," Brody said. "We've been a good team so far, right, Elle?"

His comment was bittersweet. They had almost been a team. A real team. The ultimate team.

A lifetime ago.

"We can do it," she said, keeping her eyes focused on her friend. She was afraid to look at Brody. Afraid that he might see the longing on her face, might realize the truth that she'd regretted leaving him from almost the minute she left.

"Let's go, then," Leo said, taking the lead.

Elle followed with Brody taking up the rear. Mindful that Jamas might have people looking for them in the jungle, they did not talk on the way but tried to move quietly through the heavy growth. Twenty minutes into the trip, they did have to turn on their flashlights. Leo had his own and Brody carried theirs. Both men were careful to keep the light down, to have it shine only a few feet ahead of them. Twice they did have to resort to clearing the path. Fortunately, Leo's machete was much more effective than Mrs. Hardy's knife. It was also noisier and while Elle knew it was difficult for sound to carry through the heavy jungle, she was still worried. She'd brought danger to Brody and now Leo was involved, too.

Just as Elle was thinking that she was going to fall over from fatigue, the little house seemed to suddenly pop out of the jungle in front of them. Leo flashed his light up, allowing her a minute to inspect it. It was on stilts, with bamboo walls and a thatch roof. It was almost frightening how well it blended it with the surrounding area.

They climbed the steps and Leo opened the door. The inside was one big room. There was a small table and two chairs to the right. On the far wall was a large fireplace. That surprised her. Most of the homes in the jungle villages did not have indoor fireplaces for fear of highly flammable materials catching fire. There were two large tanks of water. That didn't surprise her. After all, water was Leo's business. There were several buckets, stacked upside down, next to the tanks.

And there was a bed, stripped bare of any blankets or sheets, but they appeared to be in the plastic container that sat on the bed. There were two other clear plastic containers on the floor and they contained dishes and silverware and pots and pans.

"The water that is inside is safe to drink and to wash in. There are towels in with the sheets."

Elle figured that was the nicest way Leo could say, *Hey, you two could benefit from a bath*. She could easily get past the gentle criticism.

"I'd suggest that you don't use the fireplace. No need to attract attention to this location. I brought a few things that don't require cooking." Leo opened his backpack and pulled out wrapped cheese, some mangoes and bananas, and a jar of peanut butter.

Elle smiled when she saw that. Leo had been having peanut butter shipped to him for years.

Her friend caught her eye and tipped the jar in her direction. "Brody bought some bread in the village. You won't starve," Leo said. "There's some wine, too." He pulled out a glass bottle with a cork stopper. "Although I suspect you're more in the mood for water."

"How long will we need to stay here?" Brody asked.

"Tomorrow morning I'll report the location of the wreckage. At the same time, I'll arrange for a flight out of the country. You won't be able to go commercial. If Jamas knows you're alive, and we have to assume he does, he surely has connections that will allow him to monitor airline-ticket purchases. I know a few pilots that I trust. It's a matter of getting in contact with them and seeing who is willing and available to help. I'll try to be back by noon with a plan. The faster we can get you out of Brazil, the better."

Brody stepped forward. "Leo, I don't think we can thank you enough."

Leo waved his hand. "Elle would do it for me. I suggest you stay inside as much as possible over the next eighteen hours. Eat, rest, replenish your fluids. That's your job."

Elle kissed her friend on the cheek. "Thank you. You are literally saving our lives."

"Happy to do it. I'll be happier, however,

when you're safely away from here. Jamas will be relentless in his search to find you."

"Who knows about this place?" Brody asked.

Leo shrugged. "I don't make a habit of telling too many people about it. However, the jungle is not nearly as isolated as many think. Even if you never see them, there are many natives. They watch and listen and see and know more than you might think. I've never been bothered by them because I'm pretty well-known in this area for my work in developing safe water systems. There's no lock on the door, but no one has ever taken the few things that I keep here."

It made her feel a bit like a goldfish in a glass bowl to think that there might be people outside the small hut. Watching. Waiting.

It was as if Brody was reading her mind when he asked, "How will they know that we're not intruders, that we have your permission to be here?"

Leo smiled. "I imagine several of the natives saw us on our journey here. I know, we didn't see them but trust me, they were there. Word will pass that I led you here." He pushed open the narrow door. "Good night. Don't worry."

Brody moved quickly, catching Leo before the door could shut. "One more thing, Leo," he said.

"Of course."

It was subtle but Elle was pretty sure that Brody used his body to edge Leo out the door. Whatever it was that Brody wanted to tell Leo, he didn't want Elle to hear. Which under normal circumstances might make her curious or even mildly irritated, but quite frankly, she was so tired and so emotionally exhausted that she didn't really care.

Whatever it was, it didn't take long because Brody was back inside the hut in just a few minutes. "Sorry," he said, "I was hedging our bets."

"Huh?"

He smiled. "I'll tell you later. I think he's a good man. I'm glad you have friends like that, Elle."

She nodded. "While I haven't known him as long, he's sort of my Ethan and Mack. Someone I trust implicitly. Someone I can count on."

Brody nodded. "There have been times in the last twenty years, when Ethan, Mack and I were all in different corners of the world, that we wouldn't see each other or even talk for months at a time. But that never mattered. We knew that we were still there for each other. No matter what."

"What would they say now if they could see you?" Elle asked.

Brody smiled. "Probably something like, *Hey, you smell. Hit the shower.*"

Elle walked over and opened the plastic tote that was sitting on the end of the bed. There were sheets, a thin blanket, two towels, two washcloths, as well as a bar of soap. "I'm grateful for everything—the food, the shelter, the water. But I'm really grateful for the soap. I feel as if the bug spray is three layers deep on me."

"Go ahead and get cleaned up. I can wait outside."

Elle shook her head. Maybe it was Leo's comment about the natives hearing and seeing everything, but she was suddenly very nervous about either one of them being outside. They would ultimately have to go out to take care of basic hygiene needs, but that should be the limit.

"We both want to clean up. We're adults, Brody. You turn your back, I'll turn mine."

He didn't say anything. Just calmly walked over to the water tanks, picked up a bucket and filled it half-full. Then he repeated the actions with a second bucket. He brought her one of the buckets and set it down at her feet. In return, she handed him a washcloth and towel. He took it without a word and returned to the other side of the room.

He pivoted on his feet so that his back was toward her. Then he started to take off his shirt.

And she watched.

He finished with his buttons and slipped the shirt off one shoulder, then the other. His back was still smooth, still tan, still masculine with finely sculpted muscle. He did have a heck of a bruise, however. It was various shades of purple, and she realized that he'd probably gotten it when the plane had crashed and the ceiling had fallen in on him.

He'd never said anything, never complained.

He unzipped his pants, started to pull them down.

Gracious, as Mrs. Hardy was prone to saying.

She turned, almost kicking over her bucket of water in the process. What the heck was wrong with her? They were dirty. They needed to wash. It was a simple human need.

The problem was, she was struggling with a much more complex human need. Ever since Brody had kissed her, she'd been imagining what it would be like if it was something more. Ever since she'd felt his erection, so tight, so perfect, she had been wanting him with a vengeance.

But she wasn't going to do one thing about it. She and Brody had had their day a long time ago. It had been a one-act play and the theater had been closed for a lot of years.

She unbuttoned her own shirt and let it drop to the floor. Then she pulled off the cami with its built-in bra. The cotton material was practically sticking to her skin. She stood naked to the waist, happy to let the warm air inside the hut wash across her bare skin. She dipped her cloth into the water, scrubbed some soap across it, and wiped down her arms, her breasts, her stomach.

She heard two soft thuds and a swoosh and figured that Brody had kicked off his boots and stepped out of his pants. Was he totally naked?

She wanted to look. She desperately wanted to peek, to take a memory of his body back with her.

Her hands were shaking and the hut seemed warmer. She unbuttoned her pants, pulled down the zipper, stepped out of them. She pulled her bright blue panties down, too. She dipped her cloth in the water and soaped it up again.

And realized that Brody didn't have any soap. There had only been one bar.

"There's soap," she said. "I can share."

Chapter Twelve

"Okay," he said, his voice sounding rusty.

She started to turn, only to stop quickly. No looking, she told herself. She again faced the wall. And took three steps back. With each step, she could feel her body responding to Brody's naked nearness. Her skin felt more sensitive, the fine hair on her arms felt alive.

She reached her right arm back. She was holding the soap in a death grip. "Here," she said.

He reached back and brushed the back of his hand across her bare buttock.

She sucked in a breath.

Neither of them moved. She couldn't even breathe.

Until finally she felt the faint stirring of air as Brody moved his body. His hand connected with hers. She released her fingers, letting the soap shift to his hand.

She heard the soap hit the floor. Brody still had her hand. He was turning her, pulling her close.

"Brody?" she whispered, her eyes on his handsome face.

His gaze was steady. "A lot of years have gone by, Elle. I don't see much sense in wasting another day."

And then he bent his head, pulled her tight into his wet, naked body and kissed her.

For a very long time.

Making her forget that she was in the middle of a South American jungle. Making her forget all about T. K. Jamas. Making her forget everything except the fact that she loved kissing Brody Donovan.

She wrapped her arms around his neck and settled in.

She felt his desire. So hard. So needy.

She felt alive.

"Brody?" she said, her voice soft.

"Yes, Elle."

"I'm glad there was only one bar of soap."

"I'll never look at soap the same way again," Brody agreed. He took a step back, separating their bodies.

He stared at her, his eyes lingering on her breasts, her hips, her legs. "You're beautiful," he said.

"I'm thirty-four," Elle protested. "I don't have the body of a twenty-one-year-old cocktail waitress anymore."

"It's even more amazing now," Brody said. He reached for the cloth that Elle held in her hand. "Let me," he said. Then he dipped the cloth in the water and gently ran it down the length of Elle's right arm. Then he bent his head and kissed the soft skin inside her elbow.

She drew in a deep breath. Held it.

He repeated the action with her left arm, spending time gently massaging her hand. Then it was a kiss on each finger.

He dipped the cloth again and this time he started at the collarbone and worked his way down the gentle slope of her right breast, using the cloth to softly rub the pink nipple.

"Ohhh." Elle sighed.

He licked the spot his cloth had just cleaned. Used his tongue to pull her nipple inside his mouth, to suck on it.

"Brody," she said, her voice sounding thin.

"Don't hurry me, Elle," he said softly. "I intend to take my time."

And he did. He washed her with long strokes, followed by quick licks and soft kisses. Her ribs. Her stomach. Her legs. Her feet.

"Spread your legs," he said, kneeling in front of her.

He cleaned her and then tasted her.

She squirmed and he held her tight.

"Oh, my," she said. And minutes later, when her first orgasm hit hard, she knew she would have fallen if he'd not had a good hold. When it was over, she bent her knees and he let her sink down onto the floor, boneless, satisfied.

He sat down next to her and wrapped an arm around her, pulling her close. "Okay?" he asked.

"That was amazing," she said. "I can't breathe," she added.

"Yes, you can. You're talking. That means you're breathing."

She let her head loll against his shoulder. "Just because you're a doctor doesn't mean you know everything."

"I know what I'm going to be doing for the next hour," he said.

She lifted her head. "And what's that?" she asked, her tone teasing.

"I'll tell you what. You make the bed while I finish getting cleaned up, now that I've got some soap. And then I'll show you."

She smiled. "Making the bed in normal situations might be a real mood killer, but I think I'd do most anything for a real bed right now."

He helped her stand up and, in the process,

let his body slide against her, let her feel how much he wanted her.

She wrapped her arms around his neck and pulled him even closer. "Make it fast," she whispered.

"Don't you worry, darling. Just get those sheets on."

ELLE VOLLMAN HAD always been a wonderful lover. Imaginative. Demanding. Tender. Playful. And when she stretched her slim body out next to his, he felt an almost overpowering need. He wanted to be inside her, to know the great joy of having her come apart in his arms.

"Nice job with the sheets," he said.

They were simple cotton, wrinkled from having been folded tight in the plastic container, but they were clean and felt heavenly. "I'm never leaving this bed," she said.

"Sounds good to me," he replied, smiling. The real world seemed very far away.

"Brody," she said.

"Yes."

"Make love to me."

And he did. And it was everything he remembered and more. A myriad of contradictions. Hard kisses and soft touches. Hot skin and cool sheets. Yielding muscle and driving force.

When he was inside her, seated deep, she

wrapped her legs around him and rocked up. He hissed through his teeth. She did it again and again until he shifted and his strokes became long and sure.

And he felt her need spike. She exploded around him and he threw back his head and poured himself into her.

HE LAY ON his side, one arm under Elle's head, the other stroking her naked body. She was on her back, her eyes closed.

The sex had been amazingly good. Perfect.

But now they needed to talk. "I suppose it's a little late to ask," he said, "but are you on any birth control?"

She didn't open her eyes. She did, however, shake her head.

Well, okay. He waited, to see if she would initiate more conversation. She had a child. She had taken deliberate and specific action to be a parent to Mia. That had to mean that she was open to the idea of children.

What would it mean if Elle was pregnant with his child?

He would want to marry her. For sure. But was he destined to repeat his mistakes of thirteen years before? Would she leave him again?

His stomach was rolling and it had nothing to do with being hungry. He was borrowing trouble. There was no reason to believe that Elle was pregnant from one hugely fantastic bout of sex. People had sex all the time without conceiving.

He was going to stop worrying about it. And he was going to stop thinking about whether it meant as much to Elle as it had meant to him.

"Are you hungry?" he asked, determined that he could steer the conversation into some normalcy.

Now she opened her eyes. "A little."

He got out of bed and pulled on clean shorts from his bag. He cut slices of cheese and bread and mango, put them on a plastic plate that he found in one of the bins and brought it over to the bed. Then he filled their empty water bottles with water from the dispenser and brought those, as well as the bottle of wine, back to the bed.

She was sitting up, with the faded cotton sheet pulled up almost to her neck. Her cheeks were pink and the worry that had been ever present in her eyes for the past three days was gone.

"A feast," she said, smiling.

"I never thought I'd look so fondly upon a mango," Brody agreed.

"When I get back to the States, I'm going to have a bacon cheeseburger. And fries. Lot of fries," Elle added.

That sounded good. "I'm going for the desserts," he said. "Chocolate cake. Maybe cherry pie with vanilla ice cream."

She frowned at him. "And you, a respected member of the medical community," she said, her tone deliberately shocked. "Have you seen the latest research on saturated fats?"

He shrugged and helped himself to a piece of cheese. "I don't care. After I have dessert, I'm going to have a steak with a baked potato and lots of sour cream."

"Now you're talking," she said, layering cheese and mango on her slice of bread.

They ate in silence for several minutes. After Elle drank her entire bottle of water, she picked up the wine bottle. "Cheers," she said. She uncorked the wine, drank and passed the bottle to him. He took a sip. It made the back corners of his mouth tighten up in response.

"This tastes remarkably similar to something that Ethan, Mack and I made in college with a bottle of grain alcohol and blackberry brandy."

She smiled. "You'll certainly have a story to tell your friends when you get back to the States. You mentioned that they're both getting married soon, right? You'll go to the weddings?"

"Yes, it's a double wedding at the McCann cabin. Mack and Hope were initially reluctant to go along with Chandler's suggestion because they didn't want to horn in on her big day, but she was insistent. Said that nothing would make her happier than sharing a wedding day with her brother."

"I'm sure it'll be wonderful," Elle said. "Have you, Mack and Ethan seen much of each other in the last couple of years?"

"We'd go for long stretches of time without seeing each other but always kept in contact with texts and phone calls. Ethan was in the army, Mack in the navy and I just retired from the air force."

Her eyes widened and she sat up straighter. The sheet slipped and he worked hard to keep his gaze eye level.

"I never pictured you in the air force," she said.

"After my residency, I worked in Boston for a couple years but I was restless. I thought about going back to Colorado, but I decided that I'd try something very different." How could he tell her that he'd always dreamed that they'd go back to Colorado together, that he simply hadn't been able to make the trip without her?

Some things were probably better left unsaid.

"I enlisted and have had several deployments to Iraq and Afghanistan during the last eight years. Fortunately or unfortunately, depending on your perspective and which end of the scalpel you're at, war presents opportunities for advancements in medicine. Dollars become available for research, and new techniques and treatments are developed. That has certainly been the case as we've tried to better respond to bodies damaged by roadside bombers."

She shook her head. "I'm so sorry. The carnage you've seen is probably staggering."

"Of course. But I also had the opportunity to witness true heroics. So many very brave soldiers. Some of whom are going home without arms or legs. Then, of course, there's the traumatic brain injuries. But still, they're determined to have a life, even if it's going to be a very different life from the one they had once anticipated."

"Thank you for your service," she said.

She didn't say it because it was the politically correct thing to say. He could tell she meant it. And it felt good that she was proud of him. He ate a slice of bread, not sure how to tell her that her opinion mattered.

"How about you?" he asked instead. "I know that you're teaching now but what did you do before that?"

She picked at the hem of the sheet and looked toward her feet. "I lived in Paris for a few years and worked at odd jobs. I make a mean latte," she added, looking up. "Then I moved to Peru and worked as a nanny. The husband and wife were both high up in the government and they had three children. While I was working for them, I finally finished college." She made eye contact. "Took me long enough, I know. I imagine you never thought it would happen."

He shrugged. Elle was one of the smartest people he'd ever met. He'd never even considered that she wasn't smart enough to go to college. He'd figured she just wasn't interested.

"Anyway, after the youngest started school, I moved to Brazil and started working at the school, teaching English. I loved it."

"And that's where you met Jamas?"

"Yes," she whispered. "He was a great benefactor to our school and to several others. I had no idea that he used his access to our students to pick out his next victims."

"How did you find out?"

"Mia told me. I'm not sure why he targeted Mia. Perhaps because she's such a beautiful girl. Perhaps because I'd adopted her and maybe he was trying to hurt me. What I learned from the authorities recently is that they believe he tries to make it look as if the girl is a runaway with fake notes and other clues."

"Bastard," Brody said.

"Absolutely. He played on the emotions of

these young girls. He had several women working for him. Why they would do this, I have no idea, but they would make contact with these young girls, giving them small gifts at first to earn their confidence. You have to understand, these are very poor children with many needs and wants. Once they accepted, they were of course warned to tell no one, that they and their families would be in trouble for accepting the gifts. That's nonsense, of course, but adolescent girls don't understand that."

"Of course not," he said. "Oldest trick in the book."

"Once their confidence was earned, the women would use some excuse to get the children into their vehicle and they were taken somewhere. Based on what I now know, they would be sold within hours and moved out of the country, never to be heard from again."

"You said that Jamas made a mistake with Mia."

"Yes. Evidently several different women tried to entice Mia into accepting gifts, but she would accept nothing. Maybe Jamas became intrigued by the challenge. Once he told me that he fancied himself a collector of all things rare and beautiful. At the time, I thought he was talking about art," she admitted.

"For whatever the reason, he was obsessed

with Mia," she went on, determined to forgive herself for not realizing sooner that Jamas was a monster. "He made contact himself, figuring that Mia would trust him because he was a frequent visitor at the school. He made a mistake, though. The gift he gave her was a fashionable fragrance, one that all the girls saw advertised in the magazines that they devoured. When Mia saw that, she realized it was the same thing that she'd seen in her friend's backpack, just a week before the friend had suddenly run away from the orphanage."

"She associated the fragrance with her friend's absence?"

"She knew her friend would never have run away, because there was a family that had expressed interest in adopting her. Mia was very grateful to have been adopted. She knew that this girl also wanted to be adopted more than anything. Mia connected the fragrance and the girl's unexpected leaving and came to me. Thank God she trusted me enough to tell me."

"What did you do?"

"I had to be sure. I arranged a party at the school, a fund-raiser, and invited all the donors from previous events. Jamas was on that list. He came and I made sure there was an opportunity for him to talk with Mia. He gave her another gift, a signed photo of a popular band in Brazil."

"Something that most adolescent girls would see as valuable."

"Exactly. When he gave her the gift, he told her that he had something even more special that he wanted to show her and that his sister would pick her up from school on Monday of the following week. I wanted to confront Jamas but I knew that it would be a mistake. I didn't know who I could trust. He's a very power-ful man with ties to the local police and gov-ernment. I conferred with Father Taquero and at his suggestion, I contacted the FBI. At that time, I thought these were kidnapping cases. Let's just say that my inquiry sparked quite a bit of notice. Within hours, I had talked to sev-eral people from different agencies. I didn't re-alize it but Jamas was a known figure to many, but no one had been able to personally connect him to any crimes. He had made a big mistake in approaching Mia directly."

"What happened next?"

She hesitated and he got scared. "What hap-pened, Elle?"

"I had been assured that only a very tight cir-cle of people were aware that I had contacted authorities. But the next night, I was attacked on my way to see Father Taquero. Two men were pulling me into a waiting car when Father Taquero and his dog, his very big dog, came around the corner. One of the men got bit and the other tried to shoot the dog. But by that time, we had attracted some attention and the men drove away."

Brody felt a chill run down the length of his body. Elle had been manhandled by goons and likely would have been killed. Lost to him forever. He had never been a particularly violent man, but he was filled with the urge to kill those responsible for hurting her.

She must have sensed his emotion because she didn't wait for him to ask the next question. "With Father Taquero's help, I arranged for Mia to go to a safe place that same night. No one will be able to find her, I'm confident of that. The story I told you about taking books to a teacher in Fortaleza was partially true. There are books in those boxes. There is a teacher at the school that I know. But the reason I was going there was that I had contacted the one person that I believed I could trust, told him that I thought he had a leak, and he had promised that he would meet me in Fortaleza and arrange safe passage for both Mia and me back to the United States."

"So when our plane didn't land, the person

you were supposed to meet should have immediately sensed that something might be wrong."

"Yes. That's why when I heard the helicopter, I was so excited. I figured that he had come
for me. But he would never have shot at me.
Mia and I are his key witnesses."

"What's his name?"

"Flynn O'Brien."

Brody smiled at her. "I imagine he's not
Irish."

"I suspect he is, based on the accent I heard
when I talked to him. I don't really care. What's
important to me is that he can safely get Mia
and me back to the United States." She yawned,
covering her mouth with the back of her hand.

He smiled at her and gathered up the plastic plates and the wine bottle. "You need some
rest," he said.

She nodded and slipped down in the bed.
"This could all be over tomorrow," she said.

He didn't want his time with Elle to be over.
But he wasn't sure if he was ready to tell her
that yet. First he needed to understand why
she'd left so many years before. "Elle," he said.

There was no answer. Her breathing was
steady and deep.

He settled in next to her, pulling her in tight
to his body. He could wait. He could do most
anything as long as Elle was in his arms.

Chapter Thirteen

Elle woke up feeling warm and comfortable and, oddly enough, content. That was not an emotion that she was generally up close and personal with. She'd spent a lifetime searching, looking for the thing that was going to make her feel whole, make her feel as if she'd truly left her childhood behind.

Contentment might be an elusive emotion, but right now it filled her, surrounded her, even led her to do something that she might normally not do. She turned in Brody's arms. He was awake.

"Make love to me," she said.

His eyes widened. "Well, hell," he said.

"Huh?"

"I want the last fifteen minutes back, because I spent them thinking about how I was going to convince you to let me do just that. You're easy."

"But still worth it," she countered as his lips traced her collarbone.

He lifted his head. "That, darling, is not even worthy of discussion."

An hour later, they lay in bed, him on his back, her on her side, nestled close. She was stroking his bare stomach. "We should get up," she said. "Leo said he'd be here by noon. But if he comes early, I don't want him walking into this."

Brody didn't answer. He was staring at the ceiling.

"Penny for your thoughts," she teased.

He shifted so that he could look her in the eye. His face was very serious. "Why did you leave?"

She'd expected the question. How could he not ask it? How could she not answer it now, after all this.

"The first night that you came into the bar, I noticed you. I wasn't even waiting on your table and still I noticed you. You have this way of bringing light into a room, making everything around you brighter, making everything look better. I know it sounds crazy but I could *feel* you in the room."

"You never said a word to me."

"Of course not. But I watched you. And then when you came back and I was your waitress, I thought, *Wow, he's as nice as he looks.* You were polite and funny and I heard you tell your friend to clean up his act after he let loose an F-bomb in front of me. And you left very generous tips."

"I was trying to get your attention."

"You had it. And when you asked me out, I couldn't believe it. And I meant it when I said no. But you were persistent and…it was probably wrong but I wanted what you were offering, I wanted a chance to be *that* girl. The girl with the incredible boyfriend that everybody admired and respected. Even if it couldn't last."

"But—"

She held up a finger, stopping him. "You amazed me. So well educated, so confident, so emotionally whole. I would lie in bed at night and think, how does one get to be Brody Donovan? Then when we visited your parents over the holidays and I saw how perfect they were, it made sense to me. You were destined to be perfect. Destined that everything you did or touched for the first twenty-five years of your life would be golden."

"You left because I had a good life?" he asked, unable to keep the disbelief out of his tone. "Because I had nice parents?"

"No. Of course not. I left because I saw how different we were. How different we would always be."

She saw the look on his face and knew that he was never going to understand unless she told him the truth, the whole truth. "Brody, I grew up in a series of trailer parks."

"It's no crime to be poor, Elle."

"You're right." She swallowed hard. "When I was twelve, I was molested by my stepfather. He touched me. Made me…touch him. Do things to him."

She could see the shock, the revulsion, on his face. "Rivers?" he asked.

"Yes."

"I hope the bastard spent time in jail," he said.

"No charges were pressed even though it happened many times. I told my mother and she didn't believe me. She said that if I told anyone else, we would all be in big trouble."

"How could she say that?"

"I don't know. At twelve, I didn't understand how wrong it was for her to respond that way. I did know that I hated what Rivers was doing to me. I lived in constant fear that my bedroom door was going to open. I stopped sleeping, I was failing school."

"What happened?" he asked, his voice subdued.

"A teacher contacted a social worker, who called my mother. I don't think my mother ever admitted to the social worker what was happening, because Rivers was never arrested. But it evidently scared my mother enough that she decided that she and I were leaving. That night we packed the car while Rivers was working second shift at the factory. I was so grateful that I didn't ask many questions. It was only years later that I realized that we left because my mother was afraid that she was going to be arrested because she'd allowed it to happen."

"I'm...so sorry," he said.

She could see the distress on his face. She put a hand on his cheek. "It's okay. It's over. It's been over for a long time."

He didn't respond. Probably because he knew her words were empty. Things like that were never really over.

"We moved to Utah. To another trailer park. My mother said she wasn't angry with me, but I knew she was. She blamed me."

"You know that's ridiculous?" he said.

"I do now. At twelve, I figured she was right. She and Rivers got divorced and my mother never remarried. I think that somehow she blames me for that, too. That she's had to spend her life alone because of me."

"Just because a person is an adult, it doesn't mean she has mature thinking skills," he said.

"Very true. It was a difficult environment to

live in. I quit school when I was sixteen and left home."

She stopped and looked at him expectantly.

"That was probably a really scary thing to do," he said.

She waved a hand impatiently. "Brody, I never graduated from high school. You were already in med school, about to graduate at the top of your class, and you were engaged to a high-school dropout. I always made a joke about not being ready for college. It had nothing to do with being ready. I couldn't enroll because I didn't meet the minimum entry requirements."

"I wouldn't have cared," he said. "I would have helped you."

She shook her head sadly. "I wanted to tell you. When you asked me to marry you, I told myself that I deserved you and all the happiness that you'd brought into my life. But then you started interviewing for positions. A couple of the hospitals invited us to dinner. And I realized that in the world that you were entering, people would make judgments about you based on their impressions of me."

"You made a wonderful impression. Everyone loved you."

"I have a criminal background, Brody. I was arrested six days after I turned eighteen. I spent thirty-two days in jail."

He swallowed hard, probably because he wasn't totally unaware of what young girls on the street did to earn money for food and shelter. "For what?"

"I vandalized a man's car. I was working at a bar. Those are the only jobs a young girl without a high-school diploma can get. This guy kept coming on to me. Wouldn't take no for an answer. One night, after he'd put his hand up my skirt, I went a little crazy. I took bottles and bottles of alcohol and broke them open inside his vehicle. The interior of his Audi was a mess of broken glass and liquor."

"He deserved it, Elle. He was a jerk. And it makes sense. You had a history of abuse. It was no wonder that you reacted that way to unwanted advances."

She shrugged. "There were too many things. At some point, at some time, it was all going to come out that Dr. Brody Donovan was married to a high-school dropout with a criminal record. I could not be the first not-perfect thing in your life. I could not let the man who never made a mistake make a real whopper. I just couldn't."

BRODY WAS STUNNED. Speechless. She'd left to protect him.

He stood up and walked around the small

room. He felt as if there was energy bubbling up in his body and that the top of his head would blow off if he couldn't expel some of it. His heart was pounding in his chest.

The thirteen-year-old mystery was solved. She hadn't left because she didn't love him enough; she'd left because she loved him too much.

It had never seemed more important to say the right words. He stopped walking and faced her. Her face was pale and streaks of fresh tears ran down her cheeks.

She was beautiful.

"Elle, I am not perfect. And I'm sorry that you ever felt that you needed to be perfect for me. I don't expect that, I don't want that."

"But—"

He held up a hand to silence her. "Please, let me finish," he said. "You are very smart and probably the most courageous and giving woman I've ever met. You survived something that no child should have to survive. How you managed that, I'll never know but it tells me that you can survive anything." He shook his head at her. "You do realize that you were on your own at an age where I still needed my mother to iron my shirts. I'm the one who's not worthy."

"Don't be ridiculous," she said.

"You say that to me a lot. I don't care if I'm ridiculous. Not as long as you're there to witness it. You're an amazing woman, Elle. I thought that thirteen years ago and I still think it today. I love you, Elle."

She launched herself into his arms. "Oh, Brody. What did I ever do to deserve you?"

"We deserve each other. We're perfect for each other."

He kissed her, his tongue in her mouth, his body holding her tight. And then he backed her up until the back of her knees touched the end of the bed. He gently pushed her backward and when she collapsed, he followed her down onto Leo's wrinkled sheets. And he made sweet love to her.

WHEN ELLE WOKE UP, she could feel the jungle heat seeping into the small hut. Brody was cutting slices of mango, arranging them on a tray with hunks of cheese and bread.

"Hungry?" he said, turning toward her.

"Yes. I'm still having thoughts of cheeseburgers and fries," she said.

He shrugged. "I'm sorry. That's what they're having in the hut next door. You, unfortunately, landed in the fruit, cheese, bread and peanut butter hut."

"Better than the Brussels sprouts and egg-nog hut."

"For sure." He handed her a piece of bread with peanut butter. "Once we land in the States, I'll take you for a cheeseburger and fries. Maybe a chocolate shake if you're really nice."

They'd talked a lot about what had brought them to this place but not much of what was next. As horrible as the trek through the jungle had been, these last hours had been an almost miraculous interlude, something that she had never anticipated, never even hoped for, because it just wasn't going to happen.

But it had. And it would soon be over. "What are your plans when you get back to the States?" she asked.

"I have a job waiting for me in San Diego. I'm joining a group of orthopedists. I hope that I never see another bombing victim." He ate a piece of cheese. "What about you?"

"I need to find a place for Mia and me to live. Then get her enrolled in a school. Then find a job." She smiled. "I guess I have about a thousand things to do, all equally important."

He stared at her and she felt herself get even warmer. His gaze was intense. "San Diego has really great weather—good for a kid who is used to a warm climate with lots of sunshine.

I mean, you wouldn't want to go to Seattle or Buffalo or someplace like that."

His tone was challenging. "I wasn't thinking Seattle or Buffalo," she said.

"San Diego has the ocean, too. And a great zoo. I'm sure there are some wonderful schools for Mia and probably lots of jobs for teachers."

What the heck was he saying? Did he want her to come to San Diego? Did he want her and Mia to be with him?

"I guess there's more to San Diego than I realized," she said. "Maybe I should check it out."

"I wish you would," he said, his voice cracking at the end. He cleared his throat. "You and Mia could stay with me. While you're looking," he added.

Baby steps. He was acting as if they should take a few baby steps after they'd run the 100-yard dash in less than five seconds. But he was right. The sweaty jungle sex, even if it had been spectacular, had been serendipitous. Living together, making a life together—that required careful planning, careful consideration.

It was enough to know that he wanted to see her again, to meet Mia. It was enough to know that somehow he'd found a way to forgive her for all the hurts she'd inflicted upon him so long ago.

It might take a little longer for her to forgive herself. She'd never considered that Brody would question that she hadn't loved him. She'd been so wrapped up in doubting that she was good enough that she hadn't even considered that he might question his own worth.

It said something that Brody, so confident, so smart, so damn together, had come a little undone. And that something gave her the confidence to say what definitely needed to be said.

"I'm sorry for what I did thirteen years ago, Brody. It was selfish and inconsiderate and I don't blame you for being very angry with me."

He shook his head. "Everything happens for a reason, Elle. We were together and then we were apart and now we've found each other again. All of that happened for a reason."

"It's almost noon. Leo should be here shortly," she said. "I'm going to step outside," she said, "and take care of some things. Fortunately, it appears that I am fully rehydrated."

"Be careful," he said.

"I won't go far," she promised. While she hated to do it, she slathered on mosquito repellant. Even a short time outside warranted some protection.

When she opened the door, the oppressive humidity and heat of the jungle hit her hard. She climbed down the steps and walked twenty feet into the trees. She looked around before squatting and taking care of business. She was pulling up her pants when she heard a noise off to her left. She advanced toward the edge of the tree line cautiously.

There was a man, heavily armed, approaching the hut.

Leo was not with him.

She had no idea whether he was friend or foe. All she knew was if he was the enemy, she was not going to let him surprise Brody.

There was really only one alternative.

"Hello," she said, her tone as confident as she could manage under the circumstances. "May I help you?"

BRODY HEARD THE three quick knocks followed by a sharp, separate knock. He picked up Mrs. Hardy's knife and carefully opened the door. He saw the man first, then Elle, and his heart rate shot up.

"It's okay," she said, reaching out for him. "Friend of Leo's. We met up outside." She turned back to the men. "This is Brody Donovan. Brody, meet Bob."

The dark-skinned man nodded and murmured hello in a very thick accent.

Brody would bet his last nickel that his real name wasn't really Bob.

"We have to go," the man said. "Leo has arranged transport and will meet us at a small airfield about ten miles from here."

Brody looked at Elle. Ten miles in the jungle was a long way. "We're walking?"

"Only for the first mile. We'll take river transportation for most of the trip, finishing up with a half-mile walk."

"You have a boat?" Elle asked.

Bob shook his head. "This particular river is too shallow for motorized craft. We have a sturdy raft." His voice was deep. "I brought you a few things to wear."

The things included drab-colored shirts and pants, much like Brody had seen people in the village wearing. There were hats for both of them.

"It is better if others do not realize that there is a woman with us," Bob said.

"No problem," Elle said. She pulled on new clothes. The pants were too big, but she rolled them at the waist. She put on the hat, tucking her short hair up inside the band.

Brody knew that up close, her fine features

would never pass for a man's, but perhaps from a distance, others might be fooled. He pulled on his own new clothes and put his hat on.

"You don't exactly look as if you're out for a pleasure ride on the river," Brody said, his eyes on the guns that the man wore strapped across his chest.

Bob pulled out another big shirt from his bag. He pulled it on. "I have someone loading the raft right now with freshly picked fruit. We are going to look like three farmers, taking our crop to market."

Brody smiled at Elle. It could work. It had to work. "Do you know if Leo reported the plane wreck?"

"Yes. I suspect help is already on its way to your friends."

They walked single file, Bob in front, followed by Elle, then Brody. Brody smelled the river before he saw the narrow stretch of muddy water. It was twelve, maybe fifteen feet wide. There were dead fish floating near the shore. "Glad we boiled the water," he said to Elle, under his breath.

"That's why the work that Leo does is so important. Look," she said, nodding toward the river. "I think that's our ride."

It was a flat bamboo raft, maybe eight feet

wide and twelve feet long. There were crates of fruit on both sides, keeping it balanced.

"What do you think?" Brody asked.

"I can't think. I'm too busy trying to walk like a guy," Elle whispered.

Brody smiled. Even in the grimmest of situations, Elle could make him laugh.

They got on the boat. He turned to help Elle but dropped his hand. He probably wouldn't help another guy.

There were four long poles, attached to the raft by thick rope. Bob untied and distributed three of them. He motioned for Elle to join him on his side and Brody took the other side.

It took Brody a couple minutes to get the swing of sticking his pole in the water, deep enough that he could touch the bottom, and then pushing off.

"On the count of three," Bob said, when it became apparent that both Brody and Elle needed a little direction. Fortunately, the river had a slight current that was flowing the same direction they were trying to go.

They got the hang of it pretty quickly and were making good progress. While it was hard work, it was still infinitely easier than fighting their way through the thick jungle. About ten minutes into their trip, Brody glanced over at Elle. It didn't matter if she was dressed in rags and swaggering around like a sailor—she was simply the most beautiful, sexiest woman he had ever met.

The past eighteen hours had been amazing. And she'd seemed receptive to the idea of staying with him in San Diego while she looked for housing. If he had his way, she wouldn't need to find a house. She and Mia could move in with him. They could find a good school for Mia and if his condo wasn't big enough, they could look—

He heard the bullet right before he saw Bob crumple to his knees. Brody lunged for Elle, grabbed her around the waist, pulled her down to the deck and lay on top of her. He could hear bullets hit the water, the raft, the crates of fruit.

He lifted his head.

Bob had been hit in the upper thigh. His pants were already soaked with blood. Still, he'd ripped his shirt open to get to his gun and he was firing toward shore, trying to protect them. Brody felt a bullet skim past his ear, so close that had he not bent his head at the last minute, he'd have caught the round in his head.

"Stay down," he said. He needed to help Bob. He got up but stayed low, crouching behind the crates of fruit.

Too late he realized that the threat was coming from both sides.

"Drop the weapon. Or we will kill her."

Chapter Fourteen

The accent was heavy, the cadence fast, but Brody understood. He also had excellent peripheral vision and he could see the two men who had waded out from the opposite shore of where the attack had originated. They both had their guns pointed at Elle.

The taller one boarded the small raft, causing it to sway in the shallow water. The other man, younger and shorter, maybe not much over five feet, grabbed the tie rope on the raft, keeping them from moving with the current. He started to pull them to shore.

The tall one yanked on Elle's arm, pulling her up. She stumbled to her feet. Her face was white.

Brody fought the urge to lunge and tear the man's arm off at its socket. *You were always so smart.* That's what Elle had told him. He needed to be smart now.

"You have caused us a great deal of trouble,"

said the man holding Elle's arm. He shook her hard enough that her head jerked back.

Was this Jamas? Now that he was closer, Brody could see that the man was older than he'd first thought. His patchy beard was gray. Brody guessed him to be in his sixties.

Elle had said that Jamas was in his early forties.

"Who are you?" Elle asked.

"Shut up or I will kill you where you stand."

Not Jamas for sure. Someone who worked for him, then. Who else wanted Elle dead?

If T. K. Jamas was not with the group, they would need to take Elle to him. The man was bluffing. He didn't intend to kill Elle.

Patch, as Brody dubbed him, waved his arm in the air and three other men emerged from the heavy tree line. One of them was swaying and Brody could see beads of sweat running down his face. He had his left forearm pressed against his abdomen, but Brody could still see the growing ring of fresh blood. Bob had landed a shot.

Five all together. One injured, but still the odds were not in their favor, because these men were all heavily armed and all he had was Mrs. Hardy's knife in his pocket.

"Who are your friends, Elle?" Patch asked.

She glanced impersonally in Brody's direction. "He told me his name is Brody. Our plane crashed. He was the only passenger in good enough shape to walk for help."

She was trying to help him. The hell with that. Except that her plan was good. If they knew there was a personal connection between the two of them, they would use it against them.

It was a risk, however. Would they realize that she was lying? Did they know that the two of them had spent the night together at Leo's?

Brody waited, his breaths so shallow that he was surprised he stayed conscious.

Patch shrugged. "You have bad luck," he said to Brody. Then he ignored him and moved on to Bob. "Who is this man, Elle?"

"I don't know his name. My friend Leo hired him to take us upriver."

Brody understood what she was doing. The men had been waiting for them. That wasn't happenstance. Somehow they'd known that they were going to be on the river. That meant that information had leaked into the wrong hands. Into Jamas's hands. She no doubt was figuring that these guys had to know something about Leo.

The man looked satisfied.

She'd played it right.

But Brody realized it didn't matter when the short man still in the river started chattering in what Brody assumed was Portuguese. By the look on Bob's face, it wasn't good news for the rest of them. Patch nodded and the short man raised his gun and pointed it at Brody.

His finger was on the trigger.

"WAIT. I'M A DOCTOR. I can help him." Brody pointed to the man holding his gut.

Patch held up his free hand, stopping the shooter. "How do I know that you are telling the truth?" he asked Brody.

He was going to follow Elle's lead and give them as much of the truth as he could. "My name is Dr. Brody Donovan. I've been a physician for over ten years and I'm a board-certified orthopedic surgeon."

He saw the man's eyes change and a speculative look settle in them. It gave Brody the courage to keep going.

"I can help your man," Brody said. "He's got a bullet in his gut. It may have nicked his spleen or some other organ. I need to examine him, but I can't do it here." He wasn't sure how much English the man understood, but he made sure his tone was authoritative, as if he was used to being in charge, giving orders.

Patch seemed to make his decision quickly. He pointed at Elle and Brody and said something in Portuguese to the short man, who shrugged and switched his gun to Bob.

"You have been exceedingly helpful, but your time is up," Patch said.

Had the information leaked through Bob? By the look on Bob's face, Brody didn't think so. Everything about him, from the blazing hate in his dark eyes to the tenseness of his stance, screamed that he wanted to rip Patch's head off.

"I wouldn't help you. I've never helped you," Bob said.

Patch chuckled. "You're very stupid, you know." He nodded at the shorter man, giving permission for him to shoot.

"No," Brody said quickly. He had to take the chance. This man had risked his life to help him and Elle. "I don't know what your issue is with her, but as far as I'm concerned, everybody goes. Or I don't go."

There was some dialogue between Patch and the short man, with the short man furiously shaking his head. But Patch was clearly in charge, because finally he held up a hand, stopping the conversation. "If he makes one wrong move," he said, looking at Bob, "I will shoot him."

Bob showed no reaction to that, but Brody could see Elle's chest rise and fall with the deep breath that she took. It wasn't a huge victory, but somehow all of them were going to make it off the raft.

"It's time to go," Patch said. "The boss is not a patient man." He looked at Elle. "And you have made him angrier than I have seen him in a long time."

The other men spoke quietly to one another, nodding frequently, leaving Brody to speculate that when Jamas was irritated about something, it wasn't good for anyone.

Patch stepped closer to Brody. "I do not trust doctors. They live in their fancy houses and they do not care that they make many mistakes." His tone was challenging.

Brody didn't think backing down was in his best interest. The man was a bully, and bullies thrived on intimidation. "I haven't lived in a fancy house for a long time and I don't make very many mistakes," he said.

Patch shrugged, as if he couldn't care less. "Just know this, my new friend. If either of the injured men dies, it proves you are not a good doctor and of no use to me. You will be next."

Brody knew that he'd be lucky if both men didn't bleed to death before they got someplace where he could render treatment. A walk through the jungle was a death sentence for all of them.

He looked at Bob. "I need to stop the bleeding," he said.

Patch looked at his watch. "Two minutes."

Brody moved quickly. A quick look at Bob's leg told him everything he needed to know. The bullet had entered in the front thigh and gone through, leaving a slightly larger, more irregularly shaped exit wound.

Brody took off his shirt, scrunched it to make a rope and then wrapped it tight around Bob's thigh, just inches above the wound. It would slow or stop the bleeding. It was the best he could do.

The man was pale and his face was drawn in pain, but he did not cry out or complain. He breathing was steady.

Brody took a quick look at the other injured man. He was in worse shape. He was very pale and his breathing was short and fast. There was lots of blood on his shirt. "We need to put pressure on his wound," he said.

Patch released Elle's arm long enough to rip at the big shirt she was wearing. Buttons flew. "Use this," he said.

Elle hurriedly took the shirt off and tossed it to Brody. Brody got off the raft, which was now at the shore. He took a quick look at the man's wound and then quickly wrapped the shirt around his torso and tied it tight.

It would be a miracle if the man didn't die before they got to wherever they were going.

"Neither of these men can walk," he said. "We need to help them."

Patch pointed at his two healthy men that they should assist the man who'd been gut-shot. He let go of Elle's arm and pushed her toward Bob. "Help your friend," he said.

Brody and Elle each took a side, with Bob sandwiched between them. "Lean on me," Brody said. "Use Elle for balance."

The short man led the group, machete in hand. Then the gut-shot man with his two helpers. Then Brody, Bob and Elle. Finally, Patch brought up the rear. He walked with his gun pointed at Elle's back.

Fortunately, they didn't have to walk far. They went less than a quarter of a mile before they came upon a clearing and a waiting helicopter with a pilot in the seat. Still, Brody knew that for those carrying the injured, it was far enough to be carrying extra weight, and for the injured, it probably felt as if it had been a ten-mile-long death march.

They were loaded into the helicopter and Brody immediately went to work assessing Jamas's man. Now that he was closer to him, he could see that he was probably no more than twenty although his young face and body already showed signs of wear and tear.

He untied the makeshift tourniquet and peeled back the man's bloody shirt. He gently turned him to look at his back. No exit wound. The good news was that he wasn't bleeding out from the back. The bad news was that a single bullet could do a lot of damage to multiple organs. If he didn't open him up and retrieve the bullet, the kid was going to die for sure. If nothing else, the infection would kill him. "What's your name?" Brody asked.

"André," the man whispered through his crooked teeth.

"Okay, André," Brody said. "You're going to make it. Just hang on." He couldn't do much for him while they were on the helicopter. Brody looked up at Patch. "How long is the flight?"

"Not long. Fifteen minutes."

ELLE WAS SICK at the idea of coming face-to-face with T. K. Jamas. But she was not going to come apart now. Not when Brody had been so amazing. He'd been just seconds away from his own death when he saw the one card that he held that made him different.

And for whatever reason, it had been the right card. She'd felt the physical reaction the man had when Brody said he was an orthopedic surgeon. The energy had run through his body, down his arm and into his hand that had been still tightly clamped around her arm.

The only logical explanation was that someone in Jamas's camp was injured or sick and needed health care. Physicians were certainly available in Brazil—there were many fine ones. There had to be some reason that the person wasn't seeking help from a more traditional source.

Maybe Jamas was dying. She could only hope.

It wasn't long before the helicopter landed in an open space and the group was hurried into a one-story wood frame house that seemed to literally grow from the exterior of the mountain. It had dark green siding and a green roof.

Once she was inside, she could see that the inside was much plusher than the exterior. It was larger than it appeared from the outside and she realized that it must extend deep into the hillside, safe from prying eyes from above.

They were led to a large room in the center of the house. It had a gleaming hardwood floor and beautiful rugs. There were oil paintings on all four walls, and lovely chandeliers hung from the ceiling. They were electric, which told her that there were likely generators pumping electricity into the house. Even Jamas was not powerful enough to have had electricity run into the jungle. Well, maybe he was powerful enough, but given the exterior and how it blended into the surrounding area, she doubted he wanted to draw that much attention to this property.

Oh, God. Was this where he brought the young girls?

Jamas was sitting on the brown leather couch in the middle of the room. He was holding a cup and she suspected it was tea. On more than one occasion when he'd visited the school, before she realized he was a monster, she'd brewed him a cup.

He did not get up when they entered. He did not look ill. If he didn't require a doctor, then who?

The man who had done the talking at the river grabbed her arm and yanked her to the front. She was going to have a hell of a bruise.

That was going to be the least of her injuries given the look in Jamas's eyes, and she felt the fear that she'd managed to keep at bay rocket up.

He wasn't a man who took risks.

But he'd given instructions to bring her to him alive. Which told her that he was confident that whatever he had planned for her, she would never testify against him.

She remembered what she'd learned when she contacted the authorities. It was believed that Jamas had been involved in human trafficking for years. The girls were whisked out of the country and sold to the highest bidder, to be at his mercy. To be used, abused.

She would rather be dead.

But first she needed to do what she could to insure that Brody and Bob were able to escape. Brody was certainly holding up his end of the bargain. He'd kept everyone alive so far. She had attempted to catch his eye once or twice before realizing that he was deliberately not looking at her or appearing to be too interested.

Jamas looked at the man holding her arm. He spoke in Portuguese. The only part that Elle really caught was the man's name. Felipe.

They were talking and assessing Brody. Brody met their stare. She heard Felipe say Brody's full name, then something else, and finally *orthopedic surgeon.*

Jamas got off the couch and walked toward Brody. He carried his tea with him. "I have resources, Dr. Donovan, that will tell me very quickly whether you're lying or not."

Brody shrugged. "I'm not lying. Brody Donovan. Grew up in Colorado. Went to medical school at Harvard in Boston. Did my residency at Mass General. For the last eight years, I've been in the air force, working as an orthopedic surgeon in Iraq and Afghanistan."

Elle could almost feel the energy radiating off Jamas. He was excited about something. It was eerily similar to Felipe's reaction.

"Felipe tells me that he's given you a challenge. You get to live awhile longer if you can save these two men."

"That's my understanding, but my chances are getting worse by the minute," Brody said. "These men need treatment. Now. I need a place to work."

Jamas smiled. "There is a clinic in the basement that I believe will suit your needs. And a nurse who can assist. But first things first." He walked back to the couch but did not sit. He stood in front of Elle.

"I want to know where Mia is," he said.

"I don't know," she replied.

He gently set his teacup down on the table. Then he hit her so hard across the face that she would have fallen down if Felipe had not still had his hand clenched around her arm.

"I will ask you one more time," he said, his tone insincerely polite. "Where can I find Mia?"

She shook her head.

He punched her in the stomach. Air burst out of her lungs and she bent double.

"I can see we are getting nowhere," he said. He walked over to a side table, pressed a button and spoke in Portuguese.

Less than a minute later, a woman entered the room. Probably in her late thirties, with very dark hair pulled back into a low ponytail, she wore white pants and a white shirt and Elle assumed she was the nurse that Jamas had mentioned. She carried a small white box.

She opened the lid, withdrew a syringe and took a step closer. She did not make eye contact with Elle.

"Hey," Brody said, his tone agitated. "Sounds as if you two have some history, but quite frankly, I could probably use a couple pair of hands in the operating room. Can she help?" he asked, pointing to Elle.

Jamas shook his head. "I'm sorry, Dr. Donovan. But I have other plans for Elle." He motioned for the nurse.

Elle tried to wrench her arm away, but Felipe held her tight. She felt the poke and a hot burn in her arm muscle. Then she didn't feel anything at all.

BRODY WAS GOING to kill Jamas. He was going to rip him apart, limb by limb. And then he was going to take Mrs. Hardy's knife and disembowel him. He wanted him conscious for that.

Then he was going to do the same to every other one of his little army, too, starting with Felipe.

Jamas had hit her hard enough to crack a cheekbone or loosen some teeth. And the punch to the stomach had been brutal.

The man was an animal.

When Brody realized that Jamas intended to drug Elle, he'd almost blown it. Had hoped that Jamas would buy that he might need an extra pair of hands patching the men up. But either Jamas didn't care or his hatred of Elle ran so deep that nothing would sway him from his original purpose.

Only the knowledge that what Jamas seemed to really want was Mia's location kept him from ripping that syringe out of the nurse's hand. The drug might be something that would make Elle sleep or even make her ill, but Brody didn't think that Jamas intended to kill her.

Not yet.

Whatever the drug had been, it had knocked her out fast. Her knees had buckled and Felipe had half carried, half dragged her from the room. They'd gone to the right. After that, he'd lost the sound of the footsteps.

He was worried sick about her. Even if the medication didn't kill her, depending on what it was, it could still to do significant damage to internal organs, to a person's mind.

"Maria, can you show the doctor and his patients to the clinic?" Jamas asked the question as if he were a genteel host offering an opportunity to peruse the flower garden.

Maria nodded and put away her syringe.

Jamas motioned for two of his men to assist André, whom to this point Jamas had not even acknowledged. How the man inspired loyalty, Brody had no idea.

The interplay between Jamas and Felipe was odd. Jamas was clearly the boss and Felipe the employee. Felipe's attitude had been appropriately deferential, yet there'd been a subtext that Brody couldn't quite figure out.

And right now he needed to focus on other things. Brody motioned for Bob to drape an arm across his shoulder. Brody glanced at the leg. The tourniquet had been very effective in stopping the flow of blood, which meant that Bob had hit the lottery and managed to avoid any severed arteries or veins.

All they needed was for a few other things to start going their way and maybe they could escape from this hellhole in one piece.

Maria walked quickly, leading the group down a hallway. At the end, she opened a door and started down some steps.

Great. He was going to get to do surgery in the basement.

He'd done it in worse places.

But when Maria flipped the light on, Brody almost stumbled. It was amazing. In the middle of the Amazon jungle, tucked into a remote hillside, Jamas had built himself a modern clinic. It was well lit, with an exam table, a glass-fronted cabinet full of medications and two shelves stocked with medical supplies. There were boxes of gloves and a stack of what appeared to be pale blue lab coats wrapped in plastic.

Maria motioned for the men to put André on the table. They did as instructed, then took spots on either side of the door, as if prepared for the prisoners to make a break for it.

Brody settled Bob in the chair. "I'll be with you as quick as I can," he said.

He walked over and studied the medications in the cabinet. Many, many analgesics, used for treating pain. Both over-the-counter and narcotics. Hydrocodone. Oxycodone. Several different types of antibiotics. For the first time in what seemed forever, Brody felt a ray of hopefulness. In these surroundings, with these medications, he should be able to save both Bob and André.

It was his first test. Both Felipe and Jamas

seemed to want some proof of his capabilities. Jamas had pounced on his qualifications and Brody had no doubt that the man was upstairs, somehow checking out his credentials. That's why he'd told him the truth. For some reason, his medical skills were important. Jamas didn't look ill. Neither did Felipe or the other men.

But Brody was willing to bet that somebody in this house was. That was the only possible explanation.

Maria washed her hands in the small sink in the corner of the room and pulled on blue surgical gloves and a lab coat that came to her knees. Then she selected instruments from the cupboard and placed them on a tray. He watched her. It appeared that she knew what she was doing.

"Maria, do you speak English?"

"No talking," instructed one of the men in a heavy accent.

Brody threw him a glance. "A doctor needs to be able to quickly and efficiently communicate with his nurse, especially when I'm digging bullets out of people. I need to know what she understands."

The man frowned but he nodded at Maria.

"I have been a nurse for over twenty years," she said. "I worked in a small hospital near Salvador for most of that time. I have delivered babies, cut off legs and held people's hearts in my hand."

"Okay, then." He repeated the same routine as Maria, washing his hands, gloving and gowning up. Then he selected some local anesthesia from the cabinet and drew up a syringe.

"André," he said. "I'm going to remove the bullet. You'll be awake while I do it, but this will numb the area."

The young man nodded, looked up at the ceiling, and made the sign of the cross.

Brody would take whatever help he could get.

Chapter Fifteen

Elle woke up with the worst headache that she'd ever had in her life. It took effort to open her eyes. She was lying on a wooden floor in a totally empty room. She raised her hand to feel the side of her jaw and it felt as if her arm weighed a hundred pounds.

She'd been drugged. She remembered the nurse poking her and then it had been lights out.

She patted her jaw. It was tender.

Her stomach hurt, too.

But what was worse was a horrifying realization to know that Felipe, who dragged her into this room, had had his hands on her body and she'd been totally unable to protest in any way. It made her empty stomach cramp up.

She had no idea where she was or how long she'd been out. She looked at the walls. Real wood, not the thin bamboo that most huts were made of. The ceiling wasn't hatch—it was wood, like the floor. So she was likely still inside Jamas's house.

There were no windows in the room and only one door. She got up off the floor and tried to turn the handle. Locked. From the outside.

Jamas was holding her prisoner. Why the heck hadn't he just killed her? Then there would be no question that she'd never testify against him.

He'd have to kill Brody and Bob, too. The irony was heartbreaking. She'd left Brody thirteen years ago so that he would have the kind of life that she wanted him to have. Now she'd led him into terrible danger.

And she hadn't even had the courage to tell him that she loved him. That she'd always loved him.

He would try to save her. But he wouldn't be any match for Jamas. Brody had a conscience and there were things that he would not and could not do. Jamas had no conscience and the sky was the limit on what he was willing to do, what he was willing to subject his victims to.

She heard a noise outside the door. Locks flipping. The handle turned. And then Jamas walked in. He wore a clean silk shirt and pants and sunglasses, which made no sense at all. He carried a cup of tea and she suspected it was fresh because she could see steam coming off the cup.

"Well, well. The little stool pigeon is awake," he said. "How nice."

He didn't sound as if he thought it was really nice. She said nothing.

"What? No questions? No conversation? You disappoint me, Elle. You were always the life of the party."

"Where am I?" she asked.

He smiled. "Why, you're a guest at my home, of course."

"Do you lock all your guests in?" she asked, unable to keep her hatred below the surface.

Again the smile. "Only the troublesome ones. And you, Elle, have caused me a fair amount of trouble. But that's behind us. Now I am going to make a good profit on you. Maybe I'll donate a pittance of it to that stupid little school that you work at. Would you like that, knowing that you helped the helpless? You'll be a true martyr, Elle, because where you're going, your life is going to be hell. Maybe worse than hell."

She felt a chill settle in her body.

He came close and he raised his free hand. She braced herself for another hit across the face. Instead he gripped her chin hard. "Captain Ramano was a fool. He was supposed to take off and land in short order so that I could remove you from the plane. Fortunately for me, I didn't trust that he would follow directions and I made sure that his plane wouldn't fly for long. I was confident that no one would survive the plane crash. But I had to be sure. We were looking for the plane when we saw you. I'm suddenly very glad that Felipe is not a great shot. I must admit. I was very angry at first, especially when we couldn't find you afterward. And poor Felipe was worried that it might prove to be his last mistake. That even his trusted service to my father for all those years would not be enough to save him. But then he redeemed himself by finding not only you, but the good doctor as well."

"I'm so sorry to hear that you're ill," she said, her tone dripping with sarcasm. She was not going to let this man know that he intimidated her. He would revel in the knowledge. Plus, maybe it would encourage him to say why he needed Brody.

He tightened his grip. "Sassy. I'll have to make sure I include that in your information. Many men will pay extra for the chance to teach a feisty woman to be submissive."

The idea of it made her sick, but she didn't flinch. "Whatever," she said.

He smiled. "Are you even curious about how we found you?"

It had to have been through Leo. Her friend would have died before he'd willingly revealed their location, so she could only assume that Jamas had somehow forced the information from him. "I'm not sure it matters," she said.

Now he laughed. "True." He released her chin and walked toward the door. "You'll be happy to know that I let your little friend Leo live. I thought about killing him, but unfortunately, he's well-known and favored by the natives. Don't need that kind of trouble. He does need to hire better help. Bob's housekeeper has been on my payroll for years. You see, he also does some security work for the government and I like to keep my eye on what he's doing."

Leo would be sick at the thought that he'd led Jamas to Elle. He would never forgive himself.

"In addition to dusting and sweeping," Jamas continued, "she monitors the tracking software on Bob's computer that allows her to see every file, every message, every keystroke actually. Wonderfully helpful, really. When she relayed the information about your need to be accompanied up the river, she had no idea that she was giving me the best present ever. It was a brilliant stroke of good luck."

By now, Leo probably knew they had not reached their destination. She remembered what Leo had said about there being eyes in the jungle. She supposed it was possible that there could have been natives in hiding, watching everything that occurred at the river. If that information somehow got to Leo, he'd know that she and Brody were in Jamas's clutches.

He would call the authorities, perhaps both local and in the States. He would have no other choice. She did not have much faith that the local police would be of much assistance. Jamas likely made large contributions that insured that they looked the other way. If Leo could get the attention of someone in the United States, it was unlikely that they could respond in time to save them.

It was a very bad situation.

"Nothing to say now?" Jamas taunted her, his hand on the door.

"Yes," she said. "Go to hell."

Jamas snorted. "That's where you'll be. You'll be wishing you were dead. You know, if you'd just tell me where Mia is hiding, perhaps I could be persuaded to find a buyer who is a bit more compassionate."

She pressed her lips together.

"This is tiresome," he said, his tone angry. "Just wait, pigeon. Spend the little time you have reflecting upon why it's never a good idea to cross T. K. Jamas."

He left, closing the door behind him with a solid thud. She heard the locks slip shut.

She sank down onto the cold floor and drew her legs up tight. She had desperately wanted to ask about Brody, to know what was going on with him.

I love you, Brody. She willed him to hear her silent message.

MARIA PROVED TO be a very competent assistant and in less than twenty minutes, Brody had removed a bullet from André, repaired the damage to his liver and sewn up his gut. André's injuries were out of his normal scope, but he was happy enough with the results when he was finished.

The men standing at the doorway proved to be helpful when they assisted in transferring their comrade onto a cot. André was pale but alert. He gripped Brody's hand and nodded his thanks.

"You'll be okay," Brody said. It was not the first time in his life that he'd performed surgery on an enemy. That happened during war, too.

When it was Bob's turn, Brody thought he'd see significant muscle and tissue damage because the bullet had traveled all the way through the thigh. It was about what he'd expected and not all that different from many of the injuries he'd been treating for years. Brody made the repairs and sutured both the entry and exit wounds.

Bob would need months of physical therapy to regain the strength and motion in his leg. But for both men, the most immediate worry was infection. However, Jamas's selection of antibiotics was quite extensive, likely because even a scratch in the jungle could be problematic without an effective antibiotic. Maria selected one off the shelf. Brody examined the choice, agreed with it and picked up the first syringe.

Delivering the drugs intravenously was the best way to get a strong antibiotic into them quickly.

"These men need to rest," he said.

"We have another cot in the room next door," Maria said. She motioned for the men standing by the door to move André's cot to the other room. When they returned, they linked arms and carried Bob out of the room. When they were out of earshot, Brody took his chance.

"You're a good nurse, Maria. What are you doing here, working for Jamas?"

The woman looked over her shoulders, as if to make sure that she would not be overheard. "It's not a terribly complicated explanation," she said, her tone sad. "Jamas pays three times what I could make working somewhere else.

My sister and her husband were killed in a car accident two years ago. My mother is raising their four children. My financial contribution is very helpful. Plus I am able to go see the children once a month."

"Those are good reasons, but you have to know this isn't right. He's going to kill us, isn't he? You've seen it before."

Maria did not answer.

Brody took a chance. "Will you help us? Show us a way out?"

The woman met his look, her brown eyes flat. She'd sold her soul a long time ago. "I will not help or hamper any escape efforts. That's the best I can do."

Brody heard returning footsteps. "Why does Jamas need a full-time nurse?" he asked quickly.

"You'll see," Maria said cryptically.

When the men returned, Brody was on one side of the room and Maria was on the other, tidying up the supplies.

"Now what?" Brody asked.

"So far so good," Felipe said, entering the room. With a motion of his hand, he dismissed the other two men. "Come with me, Doctor."

Felipe pointed him toward the stairs and Brody went. Instead of taking him back to the big room where they'd first met Jamas, Felipe led him down a hallway. He unlocked a door and motioned for Brody to enter. There was a single bed and a dresser with a lamp.

"You will wait in here," Felipe said. Then he left.

Brody heard the door lock engage and knew that Felipe had used a key to lock him in. He sat down on the bed. The mattress was firm and the bedding looked new. Evidently Jamas didn't entertain in this room often.

But for some reason, he'd given it to Brody. And even Felipe seemed to have a slightly different attitude toward Brody than he had initially. Certainly not deferential but there was perhaps a reluctant respect. Whatever it was, he intended to use it to his advantage.

Now it was a waiting game. How long would it take for Jamas to tip his hand?

He had to find some way to insure Elle's safety, some way to convince Jamas that Elle was necessary, without tipping his own hand that Elle mattered.

It was like walking on a tightrope over a swamp filled with alligators. One wrong move and he'd be toast.

He could not fail Elle.

Hang on. Just hang on, Elle. Be strong. Don't let the bastard win.

His bag was in the corner of the room, on

the chair. No doubt someone had searched it by now. There was nothing in there to see. He had Mrs. Hardy's knife in his pocket still. He fought the desire to reach in, to touch it, to feel the sharp point. But he didn't. He would be surprised if the room was not monitored. Probably for sound and there could even be a camera. He wasn't taking any chances.

Jamas wouldn't be happy if he knew that his men were sloppy. They had taken Bob's gun and roughly searched him for other weapons, but they hadn't done the same for Elle and him.

He still had his matches in his shirt pocket and one other ace up his sleeve. He could feel the slight weight of the pen flare guns around the waistband of his pants. Before leaving camp that first morning, he'd grabbed the plastic bag that contained the three pen flares and thrown it into his bag.

Pen flares were easy to use. Simply screw the flare onto the end of the cylinder, aim high, pull back on the trigger and let it go. The flare could usually go a couple hundred feet in the air. But it only burned for seconds, maybe six or seven. That was why flares were generally only an effective tool if your rescuer was already in the general vicinity and you were attempting to help him pinpoint your location.

He had dropped the bag of flares on top of

his clean shirts and started to zip his bag but stopped. Something that he'd learned about flares probably twenty-five years ago from some Scout leader suddenly had popped in his head. *Always be ready.* He remembered the man telling the troop that people sometimes wore flares around their necks on a lanyard, just so they would be available fast.

Brody sure as hell hadn't wanted to be in the position of searching in his bag when an opportunity of rescue suddenly presented itself. He also hadn't wanted to take the chance on losing the flares if he somehow got separated from his bag.

So he'd taken an extra two minutes and used the needles and thread from Elle's sewing kit and stitched the plastic bag to the inside of his waistband.

Of course, that effort would likely be for naught if Leo had not been able to act upon his final instructions. Had Jamas already killed the man?

If Leo was somehow still alive, would he remember what Brody had told him outside the small jungle hut before Leo left him and Elle for the night? If he remembered, would he act upon it or would he be too scared to go up against Jamas?

If he acted upon the instructions, Brody had

no doubt of the response on the other end. His friends would want to help. But with no communication systems available, coordinating the plan was going to difficult if not impossible.

Tell them this, Leo. Exactly this. Come at the Witching Hour.

The man had looked at him oddly, but he'd nodded. Brody had not wanted to tell him anything else. While he knew that Elle trusted Leo and the man had been very helpful so far, he hadn't felt inclined to give him more information.

Ethan and Mack would know the Witching Hour.

Of course, even if they came, there was no guarantee that they would be close enough to see a flare and more importantly, that he and Elle would be in position to take advantage of a rescue effort.

Brody forced himself to breathe. One obstacle at a time. That's what he needed to deal with. So far they'd managed to all stay alive.

If it was a chess game, the next move was Jamas's.

Chapter Sixteen

He realized he wasn't going to have to wait long, because he heard footsteps coming down the hall. The lock flipped. Jamas and Felipe entered. Jamas had a cup in one hand. He was close enough that Brody could smell the scent of the strong black tea. They did not close the door. "Come with us," they said.

Brody stood up. Jamas led the way, with Brody following and Felipe trailing behind. They walked down yet another hallway. Brody was starting to get a feel for the house. It was oddly shaped, but then again, it was more cave than structure, given that it was mostly underground. The living room where they'd first met was in the center of the house and then there were multiple hallways, like spokes of a bicycle wheel, leading off from it. So far he'd been down the hallway that led to the clinic in the basement and now this one. He suspected that meant that wherever they were keeping

Elle, it was down one of the other two remaining halls.

Jamas went to the very end, the last door. He knocked.

"Come in."

It was a woman's voice. Not Elle's.

Jamas opened the door. An attractive woman, probably in her late sixties, sat in a chair, reading a book. She wore a blue robe and had a blanket over her legs. She looked up and smiled but did not speak.

Jamas kissed her on both cheeks. "My mother," Jamas said, his voice proud.

Brody nodded. Did she have any idea that her son was a horrible man?

"Evening, Rita," Felipe said. "You're looking well."

The woman smiled. "Thank you, Felipe. You've always been an accomplished fibber."

Brody wasn't sure, but he thought Felipe was blushing. Was this part of the odd relationship that existed between Jamas and Felipe? Did Felipe have some kind of thing going with Jamas's mother?

"This is Dr. Donovan," Jamas said. "He is here to help you."

Well, that solved that part of the mystery. She was the patient. Brody saw the wheelchair in the corner of the room.

"My mother has had arthritis for many years. She is in constant pain and it has robbed her of her strength and her enjoyment of life. Doctors have said that her condition has resulted in the loss of much of the cartilage in her knees and they should be replaced. She is no longer able to walk on her own, and even taking care of her own basic needs is becoming more difficult. Maria is very helpful with that, but Mother does not like having to depend on her."

"There are many good hospitals in Brazil," Brody said. "Knee replacements are a common surgery."

Jamas shook his head. "She will not go. Her husband of forty-five years, my father, died three years ago at a hospital. He went in for a routine operation to remove his gallbladder and he was dead within twenty-four hours."

Now Felipe's comment about doctors and their mistakes made sense. "But surely…"

"She will not go," Jamas repeated. "And I will not make her. But if she could have the surgery here, in her own home, that would be different."

He could do it. But even with Jamas's connections, it would likely take days before he could secure the right implants. The idea of being in Jamas's home, of Elle being in Jamas's sights for that long, was repulsive.

Almost as if he'd been reading Brody's mind, Jamas spoke again. "We have already purchased the necessary medical supplies. I have three types of knees from three different manufacturers. I had thought at one time that Maria might be able to do the surgery, but she lacks the confidence, which makes me not confident."

"There are risks to any surgery," Brody said. "With knees, there can be infection or blood clots that result in cardiac arrest or stroke."

"You need to keep my mother safe," Jamas said. "I checked you out, Donovan. You're exactly who and what you say you are."

It was time to play the final card. "I'd do the best I could. And Maria is very helpful. But I am used to having two nurses with me in the operating room. I need another pair of hands."

Jamas looked at Felipe. The older man shrugged, then said, "Peitro can help. He does not mind blood."

"Are his hands delicate and small? I need someone with small hands because I'll be working in a very tight space." It was pretty much bull that he was feeding them, but they were so focused on moving forward with the surgery that they didn't seem to realize it.

Jamas and Felipe spoke in Portuguese. After several minutes, Jamas nodded. "Earlier you asked if Elle could assist you. We will allow that."

Brody shook his head. "I only asked for her because I didn't see anybody else. I'm not crazy about the idea of working with her. Based on what I've seen so far, she's the reason I'm in this mess."

Jamas smiled. "I understand your hard feelings, but Elle will assist you."

Brody ran his hand through his hair. "Listen, I'll do the damn surgery and I'll do a good job. Your mother will be dancing in a week. But I want a little something in return. I quite frankly don't care what happens to the woman. Can we agree that you'll let me go, once you know that your mother is okay, of course? I won't tell anybody that I was ever here and you'll never hear from me again."

The two men exchanged a look. Finally, Jamas spoke. "Yes. That seems fair. You will be free to go."

It was an empty promise. Brody knew that he and the rest of the group would be killed just as soon as Jamas didn't need them anymore.

"Thank you," Brody said, hoping that he sounded genuine. Maybe Jamas didn't even think it was odd that Brody could so easily walk away from Elle without a backward glance. It was the world he lived in, where sacrifice and caring for others was simply not done.

"You will do the surgery now," Jamas said.

The sooner Brody could see Elle, the better. But he wasn't ready to make a move. If help was coming, they hadn't yet had enough time to get into place. "Has your mother eaten recently?"

"She had lunch several hours ago."

"It's dangerous to do surgery when someone has eaten, especially an older person. Only liquids from here on out and we do the surgery at eleven o'clock tonight. Before that, I will want to talk to Maria and I suppose Elle, too, about what I need from them. And we should all eat a meal. I don't want anyone passing out from hunger or dehydration during surgery."

Jamas nodded. He had probably been wanting his mother to have this surgery for years. Being delayed for a few hours, for what appeared to be a good reason, was not raising any concerns.

"Felipe will escort you back to your room."

On the way out, Brody turned toward the man. "I'd like to go back to the clinic. I want to check on the patients."

"Maria is watching them."

"I'd still like to take a look. Also, if you've got three different types of knees, I'd like to take a look at them now and identify the one I'll be working with. That will allow me to better explain the process to Elle and Maria."

Felipe motioned for him to walk down the hallway that led to the basement. When they got downstairs, Brody opened the door. Maria was indeed with the patients.

"How are they?"

"Both doing well," she said.

Good. Bob was going to have to be well enough to travel soon because they weren't leaving without him. "Thank you," Brody said.

He and Felipe went into the room with the exam table. Felipe pointed him toward the cabinet in the corner. Brody opened it and examined the contents.

Jamas hadn't been exaggerating. There were three major brands of prostheses to choose from. Brody picked one that he was most familiar with. He opened the package and examined the tibial component, then the femoral.

He left the box out and shut the cabinet doors. "So, how long have you been in love with Rita Jamas?"

He heard Felipe suck in a deep breath. "Shut up."

"Did you work for her husband?" Brody pressed.

He saw a range of emotions pass over the

man's face. Brody wasn't worried about him responding physically. He needed Brody whole, with his hands in working order. Brody waited for him to turn away, to ignore the question. But Felipe didn't.

Maybe because no one had ever asked and he wanted to explain himself, perhaps especially to someone that he intended to kill very shortly so his secrets were guaranteed to be safe. "For twenty-five years," he said. "I respected him. He was not only my employer, he was my friend."

"And somewhere along the way, you fell in love with his wife."

Felipe held up finger. "And never once acted upon it until the man was dead, even when he was unable to leave his bed for the last two years of his life. Never once. I would not do that to him and Rita is too much of a lady."

"You hate seeing her in pain."

"It has become much worse this last year. She rarely leaves her room."

"What were you going to do if I hadn't fallen in your lap?"

Felipe smiled, showing yellowed teeth. "That's an interesting way of putting it. I had other options. I had already identified the top orthopedic surgeons in Brazil."

The plan was pretty obvious. "She wasn't

going to them, but you were going to make sure that one of them came to her."

"People will generally do what you want, especially when you have a gun pointed at their wife or their child."

Brody doubted that Felipe would have lost a minute of sleep over it. Not if it helped Rita Jamas. While the plan was twisted, the devotion was admirable. And Brody was counting on it working in his favor later.

"Come," Felipe instructed. "It is time for you to return to your room. Maria and Elle will join you. You can eat and discuss and then perhaps all get some rest. I want all of you very fresh. Now you understand why it is important to me that this operation go very well. If it does not, you will all pay. Immediately."

"Understood," Brody said. "I'll keep up my end of the bargain if you'll keep up yours. I get to walk away and not look back."

"Of course," Felipe said quickly.

Brody could hardly wait to see Elle, to know that she was okay. He wanted to run down the hall, but he forced himself to walk alongside Felipe and to wait patiently while the man unlocked the door to his room. He nodded his thanks and sat down on his bed, as if he didn't have a care in the world.

Felipe left, shutting and locking the door

behind him. It was eighteen minutes before he heard footsteps coming down the hall. The door was unlocked, then opened.

And there was Elle. Looking beautiful.

The side of her face was slightly swollen where Jamas had hit her. But she looked alert and otherwise unharmed.

Her eyes lit up when she saw him, but she didn't cry out or make any other motion.

Felipe stood behind her. "Dr. Donovan needs your assistance. You will provide it to him."

"Assistance with what?" she asked.

"With surgery," Brody interjected. "A double knee replacement."

"Dr. Donovan will explain to you what needs to be done," Felipe said.

"Do I have a choice?" she asked.

Before Felipe could answer, Brody stepped forward. "Look, I don't either, so I'd appreciate it if we could just make the best of this. You got me into this mess. You could at least try to be helpful now."

She let out a sigh. "I guess I did. Fine. What do I need to do?"

"I'll walk you through the process now," he said. "Before the actual surgery, I'll show you the instruments and explain what I'll need from you."

She nodded.

"I've arranged for us to have some food. We can talk while we eat."

She walked into the room.

"Do you have any paper?" Brody asked Felipe. "It's easier if I can draw pictures to explain the process."

"I will make sure some is delivered along with your food." Felipe stepped back, closed the door and locked it.

Brody got in front of Elle and deliberately rolled his eyes, trying to tell her that they were likely being watched. She must have understood because she made no move to touch him. She sat on the chair, near the dresser. He sat on the bed.

They said nothing to each other.

It was another five minutes before Maria joined them, carrying a tray of sandwiches. There was also cut-up fruit, several different kinds mixed together, and cookies. It looked delicious. Jamas lived well.

Felipe was behind her. His hands were free. There was a second man, whom Brody recognized from the river, carrying a card table and one chair. He unfolded the table and motioned for Maria to take the chair. Elle pulled her chair up to the table. Brody sat back down on the bed.

The three of them ate. Brody watched Elle

chew, still concerned about her jaw and the blow she'd taken. But she seemed to be doing okay.

Once they were finished, Brody pushed the plates to the side. Then for the purposes of Maria and Elle and whoever else was likely monitoring the room, Brody went through the surgery process with painstaking detail. He made a big deal of identifying when he would need both Maria's and Elle's help at the same time just in case Jamas suddenly got the idea that Elle's presence wasn't necessary.

He picked up the pencil and drew a picture of a kneecap and pointed out where he'd be cutting damaged bone and the process of inserting the implants. He turned his head toward Elle. "Since you've never done this, let me shade that so you can see it better," he said.

He made a big deal of shading and erasing, then shading some more. Maria leaned back in her chair and picked up her half-eaten cookie. *I will not help or hamper.* It appeared she was living up to her end of the bargain.

He quickly wrote, "I have a plan. Tonight." He pushed it toward Elle. Saw that she read it. Pulled it back. "That's still not quite right," he said. "Guess I'm not an artist." He erased the note, then drew over it just to make sure that his words couldn't be seen later. "This is better," he said, giving her another look.

"I think I have it," she said. "I can do it."

He knew what she meant.

Plan was really stretching it. It was more of a shot in the dark.

There was no need to tell her that.

He folded his drawings and left them on the table. It was only minutes later that the door opened and Felipe entered. He motioned for Maria to leave the room. "Come with me," he said to Elle.

She got up and left without a backward glance at Brody. The door closed and he heard the turn of the lock. He lay back on the bed and closed his eyes. But he could not rest. Energy was churning within him. His timing was going to have to be perfect. He would only have one chance.

AT EXACTLY ELEVEN o'clock, Brody heard his door lock flip. When the door opened, it was Felipe. "Let's go," he said.

They walked the length of the hall and then down the stairs. Felipe led him into the same room where he'd worked earlier. Elle and Maria were already there. So was Jamas and his mother. The room had been cleaned and Brody suspected that Maria had done it. Instruments were laid out. He inspected them. Again, this had to be Maria's work and she'd done a good job.

Brody motioned for Jamas to assist his mother in getting up on the exam table that was about to be turned into an operating table once again. The woman seemed frightened to death.

He looked the woman in the eye. "I want to assure you that I'm an experienced orthopedic surgeon and that this is going to go really well. You'll be taking a walk down the hall on your new knees by tomorrow."

"I am not afraid. I am tired of living with the pain."

"I understand. You're going to be awake for the surgery, but you're not going to feel a thing. I'm going to give you a mild sedative and then a regional anesthetic. It's called an epidural. It will numb everything from the waist down. Do you understand?"

She nodded, then shifted her eyes toward Felipe. He smiled at her.

"After the surgery," Brody continued, "we'll control your pain. Do you have any questions for me?"

The woman shook her head. "I am grateful for your help."

He wanted everybody grateful and happy

and very celebratory. So far, Jamas had not played into his plan. He was going to have to improvise. "When this is over, we'll all have a drink."

"I have a glass of wine every day," she whispered, as if she was confiding some big secret.

"Good for you. I was thinking more along the lines of that tea your son was drinking earlier. It smelled delicious. My mother used to drink tea that smelled just like that."

The woman looked at her son. "T.K. has always loved his tea. His father and I were coffee drinkers. I'm sure he'd be happy to share a cup."

Brody hoped so.

He walked over to the sink and scrubbed his hands and arms. Then he pulled on gloves. He motioned for Elle and Maria to follow the same routine.

"Ready, ladies?" he asked.

THE SURGERY WENT WELL. Damaged bone and cartilage were cut away and the implants set in place, to insure that the kneecap would move fluidly and without pain. Elle held up well, and he made sure to give her small tasks to do during the surgery. Felipe and Jamas stood quietly near the wall and did not interfere.

Maria anticipated what he would need. It

almost made him angry. She was a very talented nurse. Yet she was squandering her gift on the likes of Jamas. It made no sense to him, but then again, he wasn't responsible for the financial welfare of four children.

After closing the surgical site, he stepped back. He took off his gloves and reached for Rita's hand.

"We're done," he said.

She nodded, still slightly under the effects of the medication he'd given her.

"Everything looks good," he said. He turned to look at Felipe and Jamas. "She did very well. I don't expect any complications. We'll need to watch her carefully for the next several hours. She may suffer some limited nausea from the anesthetic."

"Maria can watch her."

No, that wouldn't work. "If you prefer. She can be moved to her own room where she'll be more comfortable. She will need to be monitored for blood clots," Brody added, trying to give them something to consider.

Felipe and Jamas spoke in Portuguese. Brody was really getting a little tired of them doing that.

Their conversation was short. "Maria can clean up in here. Felipe will go with you to my mother's room," Jamas said. "I will return Elle to her room and join you later."

Brody wished he could think of an excuse to keep Elle with him, but there just wasn't anything that wasn't going to create suspicion and put his entire plan at risk.

"I'd appreciate a cup of that tea that we talked about earlier. I don't want to get sleepy."

Jamas shrugged. "I don't see why not. I think you've earned a cup, Doctor."

Chapter Seventeen

Elle and Jamas did not speak as he walked her down the hallway. She was so anxious that she felt as if she was going to jump out of her own skin.

Brody had told her that he had a plan.

Throughout the surgery, she'd been waiting for some sign, but there hadn't been anything unusual. At least not that she could see. He'd been calm, very methodical in his approach, giving direction to both her and Maria in a very gentle tone.

He'd been kind to Rita Jamas. That hadn't surprised her. Brody would not take out his feelings about Jamas or Felipe on Rita. He wasn't that type of man.

When the operation was over, she'd desperately wanted to say something to him and tell him how absolutely wonderful he'd been. She'd wanted to tell him that she loved him. She'd wanted to tell him goodbye. Because whatever his plan had been, it didn't appear to have worked out the way he'd intended.

"You'd have made a fine nurse, Elle," Jamas said, unlocking her door.

She didn't acknowledge the comment. She just walked into the empty room and stood against the far wall.

"Tell me where Mia is," he said, his voice quiet. "Make this easier on yourself."

She kept her lips pressed together.

Jamas waited.

He walked closer. Raised his hand. Slapped her across the face hard. Her head hit the wall.

"You're a fool, Elle," he said, his voice hard. "Your buyer will be here in just a few hours. Compared to him, I'm a pussycat. I'm going to get enjoyment in the future thinking about you, Elle. Imagining your life, if you want to call it that."

He turned and left the room and she heard the door lock.

She swallowed hard, afraid that she would throw up. He'd hit her on the same side as before. The already tender skin throbbed.

Time was running out.

BRODY GOT RITA settled in her bed. "I'm going to give her a little something for the pain," he said. He dumped two pills out of the bottle that he'd carried from the clinic. There was a carafe of water and a glass on her bedside table. He poured her a glass and helped her take her pills.

Felipe stood next to the bed, holding Rita's hand.

"I'll talk to Maria about the exercises she should do to aid her recovery," Brody said. "Before I leave in the morning." He had to keep acting as if he still believed that they were going to let him walk out once it got light outside.

Felipe did not respond. Brody wondered if it was possible that the man actually felt somewhat bad that Brody had held up his end of the bargain while Jamas and Felipe had no intention of holding up theirs. Did he have a conscience? Or had that slowly eroded away as he'd done one bad thing after another over the years?

After about ten minutes, the door opened. Jamas came in, carrying a tray. On it were three cups. He set down the tray and handed one cup to Felipe. "Coffee for you," he said. He handed the other cup to Brody. "And tea for you. Black tea with orange and a hint of clove," he said. "One of my favorites."

Then Jamas took the other chair, as if they were old friends visiting. "How is my mother?" he asked, before taking a sip out of his own cup.

"I think she's doing okay," Brody said, letting a little concern sneak into his voice.

Jamas sat up in his chair. "What's wrong?"

"I gave her a mild sedative before administering the epidural. Her breathing appears to be a bit labored now and she's not waking up as I'd hoped. I've seen this before with patients who are very sensitive to pain medication. It might be helpful if you talked to her. Patients can hear far into states of unconsciousness. Tell her something she'd be really interested in. Something that will stimulate her."

Jamas got up and stood next to Felipe. On the topic of Rita Jamas's health, the two men were united. They cared very deeply for her.

"Mama, it's T.K.," he said, his voice soft. "I planned our trip, you know, the one to the beach. I got us a lovely villa and they tell me the sunsets are…"

Brody tuned him out. He casually reached into the pocket of the blue lab coat that he still wore and then reached for his cup. In the process, he passed his hand over Jamas's cup.

After several minutes, he stood up and joined the men at the bed. Rita Jamas was still sleeping. It was no wonder given the medication that Brody had given her. It wouldn't hurt her, but the woman wasn't likely to be waking up for some time.

"She's not waking up," Jamas said, his tone concerned.

Brody used a stethoscope to check her lungs. "It's okay. She's breathing better," he said. "I think that worked."

Jamas nodded and backed away from the bed. He took his seat. "My mother has always loved the ocean," he said. "I do not think she would have been able to make the trip this year. But now I am confident that she will."

"There are no bad times at the beach," Brody said. He took a sip of tea and sighed in appreciation. He leaned his head back and closed his eyes.

Ten minutes later, he sensed movement next to him. He opened them just a slit.

Jamas had his hand on his abdomen, and his face had a pinched look. He said something to Felipe in Portuguese and made a quick exit out of the room.

Brody didn't need an interpreter. He knew where Jamas was headed. Where he'd be for the next thirty minutes.

Brody pulled the thermometer out of his pocket. "I'm going to check her vital signs," he said.

Felipe stepped back. Brody took Rita's temperature. Then reached into the pocket of his lab coat to pull out the stethoscope that he'd stuffed there.

He put his fingers around Mrs. Hardy's knife and turned fast. In one smooth movement, he had it up against Felipe's throat.

"Be quiet," he said. "Or I'll kill you first and her second."

"No," Felipe pleaded, likely more for Rita than himself.

"Lie on the floor," Brody instructed.

When the man did, Brody placed his boot in the middle of his back. Then he took the sheet off the bed, sliced it into strips, and used it to tie the man's hands together. He yanked Felipe to his feet and walked him over to the chair. "Sit down," Brody said. He tied his feet together, then he took his longest strip and tied Felipe into the chair itself.

Cotton bedsheets were not the strongest material, but he'd been an Eagle Scout and knew how to tie a knot that wouldn't slip.

Finally, he took a small strip and gagged the man.

The last thing he did was remove the ring of keys from Felipe's belt.

He took a final look at Rita. "Good luck with

the recovery, Rita." He hoped she'd soon be getting lots of exercise visiting her son in prison.

He opened the door a crack. He had not seen any of Jamas's other men all night and he hoped that they were safely away from the property. He ran down the hallway, knife in hand.

While he didn't know exactly which room was Elle's, he was confident he knew the hallway. He didn't think it was the hallway that led to the basement and the clinic, or the hallway that led to Rita's room. That left two. He decided that it wasn't going to be the one leading to the kitchen—too much foot traffic would go by.

He chose the remaining one and knocked on the last door on the right side. "Elle," he whispered.

No answer. He debated whether he should unlock the door, but what if it was someone else's room? It could be Maria's.

He crossed the hallway. Knocked softly.

"Elle?"

"Yes."

He was so relieved he almost dropped the keys. Now he just needed to find the right one.

It was the fourth key he tried.

He swung the door open and there was Elle. He gathered her up in his arms and pulled her tight. "Thank you, God," he said. "I was so afraid that I'd never hold you again."

She kissed him. "I love you, Brody Donovan. I've never stopped loving you." She took a breath. "I was afraid that I'd never get to tell you that. I. Love. You."

He kissed her nose. "I love you more."

"Where's Jamas and Felipe?"

"Felipe is all tied up and Jamas, well, he's out of commission, I hope. I was able to put some medication in his tea that is a very effective relaxant when used appropriately but when taken in a large dose causes bad stomach cramping and all the things that go along with that. I bought us a little time, but we have to go now."

He grabbed her hand, pulled her out into the hallway and looked at his watch. Seven minutes to two. The Witching Hour was approaching. It was something Mack McCann had thought of all those summers ago at Crow Hollow. *We'll meet at the Witching Hour.* It was code that only Ethan, Mack and Brody knew. Mack had said that most people would think the Witching Hour was midnight, so by making it two hours later, they could fool everybody.

He only needed to fool one very evil man.

"We have to get Bob," Brody said.

"Of course."

They ran down the hallway to the clinic, then down the stairs. Both men were sleeping. Brody put his hand over Bob's mouth and woke him up. The man's eyes opened.

Brody smiled and put a finger up to his lips. "We're getting out of here. Lean on us."

Bob nodded and swung his legs over the side of the cot. He could put a little weight on his leg, but it was slow going up the stairs. Brody looked at his watch. Less than two minutes remained.

Elle looked at Brody. "This is going to be hard. But we can do it. We have to."

"Honey, it's possible we might not have to walk out of the jungle. There could be a ride coming."

"What? Who?"

"Ethan and Mack. I gave Leo their numbers and told him to contact them immediately if something happened to us. He was to tell them to come at the Witching Hour, which is upon us. I was confident that with Leo's connections he could discover the location of the house. Of course," he said, not wanting to get her hopes up too high, "Leo may already be dead."

"He isn't. Jamas told me that he let him live."

Brody could feel his heart beat faster. He'd done all this on a wing and a prayer and it looked as if it might possibly happen.

"And I don't think Jamas ever found the plane. They were looking for it when they saw me in the jungle. I'm sure everyone is still okay and probably has been rescued by now."

"We're next," he said optimistically.

They moved as quickly and as quietly as they could, with Bob between him and Elle. When they got to the front door, Brody reached for the handle. He whirled when he heard a noise behind him.

It was Maria. Still in her white uniform. Her hair was down and she looked younger.

"Stop," she said.

"Maria," Brody said, his tone soft. "You said that you would neither help nor hamper."

"I know. I'm breaking my word." She pointed to the door. "There's an alarm. If you open that door, it's going to blare. You need to enter the code."

She walked over and punched in a number, then opened the door. There was no noise.

"You helped Rita," Maria said. "Besides all the other reasons I stay, I stay for her, to help her. And tonight, you gave her back her life, her independence. I kept watching you, sure that you were going to do something to harm her, to send her into cardiac arrest or something to create a disturbance. I had told Jamas not to let you operate, but he was so desperate for her to have the surgery that he insisted, saying that I should signal the minute I saw you do something questionable. But you did everything perfectly. And you were so kind to her. Thank you for that."

He grabbed Maria and hugged her. "Come with us."

She shook her head. "My home is here."

He hugged her again. "If you ever come to the States, look me up. Brody Donovan. San Diego, California. I'll hire you in a minute."

"Goodbye, Dr. Donovan," she said.

They left and Brody heard the door close behind them. Thirty steps later, they were in the trees, hidden by the trees.

"Okay?" he said, grabbing Elle's hand.

Okay? No. She was scared to death. It was dark, so terribly dark. But her heart felt lighter than it had in years. Brody loved her. Again. Still. It didn't matter which.

"I'm good," she said. Nothing was as frightening as being in Jamas's house, knowing that he intended to sell her to some monster. "What's next?"

"We wait."

"How long?"

"Not long, honey. If they're coming, it should be any minute."

"What if they don't?" she forced herself to

ask. It was the middle of the night, and they were in a dark jungle, with no idea of what direction to go, with an injured man. Danger was everywhere.

"We're going to have to try to get as far away as we can. Jamas isn't going to be in the bathroom forever. He's going to check on his mother, see Felipe, and all hell is going to break loose.

"How are they going to find us?"

"I got another plan. I need my hand back for just a second."

She heard rustling. "What are you doing?"

"Getting ready," he said. "Bob, you hanging in there? How's the leg?"

"Grateful to still have it," he said. "Thank you."

"No pro—" Brody stopped midword.

Helicopter. He could hear it.

Closer now.

He pulled the trigger of the first pen flare, sending it up. It burned bright. Was it high enough? Damn these trees.

He sent up the second one.

Yes, the helicopter was closer.

He sent up the third and final flare and was practically blinded by the searchlight that hit him in the face.

"They came," he said. "I knew they would."

ETHAN MOORE LANDED the helicopter with a light touch. Mack McCann, gun strapped across his torso, had the side door open and put a hand out to help Elle. Bob was next and finally Brody.

Brody hugged Mack and gave a thumbs-up to Ethan. "Go," he yelled, knowing that neither man could hear him over the noise.

They understood. And the helicopter started to lift off.

Brody took one last look. He pointed to get Elle's attention. The front door was open and Jamas was standing in the doorway, holding his pants up with one hand. There was a look of pure astonishment on his face.

Brody grabbed Elle and kissed her soundly.

"We getting married," he said, enunciating carefully, to make sure she got it. "I can't wait to meet Mia."

Epilogue

It was a sunny, warm June day in the Colorado mountains. Crow Hollow was normally a quiet place, but today there was activity everywhere.

A triple wedding caused that kind of commotion.

At two in the afternoon, Ethan Moore married Chandler McCann. Then Hope Minnow became Mack McCann's wife. And finally, at a little after two-thirty in the afternoon, with a dark-eyed, dark-haired eleven-year-old serving as maid of honor, Elle Vollman *finally* married Brody Donovan.

* * * * *

LARGER-PRINT BOOKS!

HARLEQUIN *Presents*

PASSION GUARANTEED SEDUCTION

GET 2 FREE LARGER-PRINT NOVELS PLUS 2 FREE GIFTS!

LARGER-PRINT BOOKS!
GET 2 FREE LARGER-PRINT NOVELS PLUS
2 FREE GIFTS!

HARLEQUIN®

super romance®

More Story...More Romance

YES! Please send me 2 FREE LARGER-PRINT Harlequin® Superromance® novels and my 2 FREE gifts (gifts are worth about $10). After receiving them, if I don't wish to receive any more books, I can return the shipping statement marked "cancel." If I don't cancel, I will receive 6 brand-new novels every month and be billed just $5.69 per book in the U.S. or $5.99 per book in Canada. That's a savings of at least 16% off the cover price! It's quite a bargain! Shipping and handling is just 50¢ per book in the U.S. or 75¢ per book in Canada.* I understand that accepting the 2 free books and gifts places me under no obligation to buy anything. I can always return a shipment and cancel at any time. Even if I never buy another book, the two free books and gifts are mine to keep forever.

139/339 HDN F46Y

Name _____ (PLEASE PRINT) _____

Address _____ Apt. # _____

City _____ State/Prov. _____ Zip/Postal Code _____

Signature (if under 18, a parent or guardian must sign) _____

Mail to the **Harlequin® Reader Service:**
IN U.S.A.: P.O. Box 1867, Buffalo, NY 14240-1867
IN CANADA: P.O. Box 609, Fort Erie, Ontario L2A 5X3

Are you a current subscriber to Harlequin Superromance books
and want to receive the larger-print edition?
Call 1-800-873-8635 today or visit www.ReaderService.com.

* Terms and prices subject to change without notice. Prices do not include applicable taxes. Sales tax applicable in N.Y. Canadian residents will be charged applicable taxes. Offer not valid in Quebec. This offer is limited to one order per household. Not valid for current subscribers to Harlequin Superromance Larger-Print books. All orders subject to credit approval. Credit or debit balances in a customer's account(s) may be offset by any other outstanding balance owed by or to the customer. Please allow 4 to 6 weeks for delivery. Offer available while quantities last.

Your Privacy—The Harlequin® Reader Service is committed to protecting your privacy. Our Privacy Policy is available online at www.ReaderService.com or upon request from the Harlequin Reader Service.

We make a portion of our mailing list available to reputable third parties that offer products we believe may interest you. If you prefer that we not exchange your name with third parties, or if you wish to clarify or modify your communication preferences, please visit us at www.ReaderService.com/consumerchoice or write to us at Harlequin Reader Service Preference Service, P.O. Box 9062, Buffalo, NY 14269. Include your complete name and address.

HSRLP13R